"Don't go in the storage area again," Helen warned.

"It sounds as if there's another crazy actor in the theater group. You children could be in danger."

"There are angry fools everywhere these days," Martha said, "and many of them carry weapons. It isn't safe to cross them."

Kayo picked up the painting and turned to leave.

"There is a door behind the curtain where the painting was," Kayo said. "From the layout of the theater, that door should open into the back of your gallery." She pointed to the back wall as she spoke. "But there isn't any door on this side."

Martha said, "Don't go near that door, dear, whatever you do."

"Stay away from the door," Helen agreed. "We had it boarded over on this side years ago, right after the murder."

Books by Peg Kehret

Cages
Horror at the Haunted House
Nightmare Mountain
Sisters, Long Ago
Terror at the Zoo
Frightmares™ #1: Cat Burglar on the Prowl
Frightmares™ #2: Bone Breath and the Vandals
Frightmares™ #3: Don't Go Near Mrs. Tallie
Frightmares™ #4: Desert Danger
Frightmares™ #5: The Ghost Followed Us Home
Frightmares™ #6: Race to Disaster
Frightmares™ #7: Screaming Eagles
Frightmares™ #8: Backstage Fright

Available from MINSTREL Books

Backstage Fright

Peg Kehret

PUBLISHED BY POCKET BOOKS

New York   London   Toronto   Sydney   Tokyo   Singapore

This book is a work of fiction. Names, characters, places and incidents are products of the author's imagination or are used fictitiously. Any resemblance to actual events or locales or persons, living or dead, is entirely coincidental.

A MINSTREL PAPERBACK *Original*

A Minstrel Book published by
POCKET BOOKS, a division of Simon & Schuster Inc.
1230 Avenue of the Americas, New York, NY 10020

ISBN:1416991077
ISBN:978-1-4169-9107-6

First Minstrel Books paperback printing July 1996

10 9 8 7 6 5 4 3 2 1

Cover art by Dan Burr

Printed in the U.S.A.

For Mark Kehret

CARE CLUB
We Care About Animals

I. Whereas we, the undersigned, care about our animal friends, we promise to groom them, play with them, and exercise them daily. We will do this for the following animals:

> **WEBSTER** (Rosie's cat)
> **BONE BREATH** (Rosie's dog)
> **HOMER** (Kayo's cat)
> **DIAMOND** (Kayo's cat)

II. Whereas we, the undersigned, care about the well-being of *all* creatures, we promise to do whatever we can to help homeless animals.

III. Care Club will hold official meetings every Thursday afternoon or whenever else there is important business. All Care Club projects will be for the good of the animals.

Signed:

Rosie Saunders

Kayo Benton

Chapter 1

"I have some shocking news," Mrs. Cushman said. The sixth graders quit fidgeting in the hot classroom and looked at their teacher.

"I'm sure you remember our art study unit last month on Rembrandt, Van Gogh, and the other master painters," Mrs. Cushman said.

Heads nodded.

"And I'm sure you remember," Mrs. Cushman continued, "our field trip to the Oakwood Art Museum."

Heads nodded again.

In the front row Rosie Saunders and Kayo Benton looked at each other curiously. What sort of shocking news could involve the art museum?

"We saw an old painting that's worth over a million dollars," said Sammy Hulenback.

1

FRIGHTMARES

Typical Sammy, thought Rosie. He was more impressed by the price than by the fact that the museum had inherited a painting by Vincent Van Gogh, one of the greatest artists of all time.

"I am sorry to report," Mrs. Cushman said, "that the Van Gogh painting we saw is a forgery."

Disbelief rippled from desk to desk.

"They paid a million bucks for a fake?" Sammy said.

"The museum had a certificate from an expert," Kayo said. "He believed it was really painted by Vincent Van Gogh."

"I heard only a brief report about this on the radio so I don't know all the details," Mrs. Cushman said. "Your homework assignment for this week is to learn as much as you can about the forged painting and bring your information on Friday."

"When I lived in Chicago," Lyle Guthrie said, "a forger was caught when someone x-rayed his painting."

"Despicable," said Rosie as she made a check mark in her vocabulary notebook.

Kayo narrowed her eyes, trying to remember the definition of Rosie's new word. "Dirty, rotten scumbag?" she whispered.

Rosie nodded. "Close enough," she said.

Because of a teachers' conference, school dismissed at noon. Kayo went home with Rosie, walking slowly in the heat that had settled over Oakwood that morning.

Just as the girls got home Sammy rode up on his bike. He slammed on the brakes, making his tires squeal.

"I won five thousand dollars in a contest!" Sammy cried.

"Wow!" said Kayo. "What did you do to win?"

"Nothing."

"How did you enter?" Rosie said. "Was it a drawing at a store?"

"I didn't enter anything. I just got a letter saying I won."

"For no reason at all, someone is going to send you five thousand dollars?" Rosie said.

"That's right. And I already know how I'm going to spend it."

"There has to be a catch," Kayo said. "Why should someone you don't know send you five thousand dollars for doing nothing?"

"Who cares why?" Sammy said.

Kayo said, "My mom says if something sounds too good to be true, it probably is."

"You're just jealous," Sammy said.

"We're just sensible," Rosie replied. "You had better read the fine print in that letter."

"Now that I'm rich," Sammy said, "maybe you'll let me join your club."

"If being rich was a requirement for our club, I would not be a member," Kayo said.

"Is your club going to help the cops find the forger?" Sammy asked.

"We've told you before," Rosie said, "our club does not help the police. We help animals."

"Ha!" said Sammy. "Then why do you keep capturing criminals?"

"It's accidental," Rosie replied.

"Someone with five thousand dollars in cash could be very useful," Sammy said. "Think it over," he added as he rode away.

After lunch the girls sat on Rosie's front steps, hoping for a breeze.

"I am melting," Rosie said. "If it gets any hotter, I'll be a little pool of liquid on the sidewalk."

"Let's go over to the shopping center," Kayo suggested, "and get an ice-cream cone. We can read all the newspaper headlines to see if there's any news about the forgery."

"I'm too hot to move."

"We'll feel better if we're active, and Bone Breath would like to have a walk."

At the sound of his name, and the word *walk*, Rosie's cairn terrier jumped to his feet and wagged his tail eagerly.

After leashing Bone Breath, they started off, being careful to keep Bone Breath on the grass so the hot sidewalk wouldn't scorch the pads of his feet.

They had walked four blocks when Kayo said, "There's Lyle. He lives in that new apartment building."

Lyle lay on his stomach in the shade, reading a book.

Rosie, Kayo, and Bone Breath walked across the grass and stopped beside Lyle.

Lyle looked up. "Listen to this," he said, and he read from his book: "A dog's nose has two hundred and twenty million cells that are sensitive to odors." He sat up and looked closely at Bone Breath's shiny black nose. "Isn't that amazing?" he said. "Your dog has two hundred and twenty million cells in his nose that are sensitive to smells."

"Then why does he always roll in garbage?" Rosie said.

Bone Breath licked Lyle's hand.

"I wonder how many smell-sensitive cells a human nose has," Kayo said.

Lyle looked in his book. "Only five million, which explains why police dogs are used to sniff out drugs, and airport security dogs smell the baggage that comes through customs."

"Maybe I have more than normal," Kayo said, "and that's why I'm allergic to ordinary things like pollen and dust."

5

"What are you reading?" Rosie asked.

Lyle showed her the cover of the book. Rosie took her vocabulary notebook out of her pocket and wrote down the book's title and author.

"Do you like to read?" Lyle asked.

"Does the sun rise in the east?" Kayo said. "Whenever she can, Rosie has her nose in a book or her hand on a pencil. Rosie's a writer."

"Kayo's a baseball player," Rosie said.

Kayo stretched her arms over her head, as if preparing to pitch.

Lyle jumped up. "Congratulations!" he cried, holding up his hand first to Kayo and then to Rosie.

The girls looked confused as Lyle gave them a high five.

"What did we do?" Rosie asked.

"You acknowledged that kids can *be* something. Right now! Not in the future. Now!" Lyle pointed at Kayo. "You said, 'Rosie *is* a writer.' You didn't say, 'Rosie's going to be a writer when she grows up.' " He pointed at Rosie. "And you said, 'Kayo *is* a baseball player.' Right now. Today. Kayo *is* a baseball player."

Lyle put a bookmark in his book. "Adults always ask what I'm going to be when I grow up," he said. "It implies I'm not anything now—just a glob of unmolded clay, waiting to turn twenty-

6

one, when I will miraculously become someone important."

"So, what are you?" Rosie asked. "Right now?" Lyle had lived in Oakwood only a month; she didn't know anything about him.

"I am a dancer and a singer." Lyle scratched behind Bone Breath's ears. "I'm also an animal lover."

"This is Bone Breath," Rosie said.

"What kind of dancing?" Kayo asked.

"Modern dance. Jazz. Some tap." Lyle kicked one leg high in the air, grasped the ankle, and twirled in a circle.

Rosie and Kayo clapped.

"I just got a part in *Pirate's Plunder* at the Oakwood Community Theater," Lyle said. "I'm one of the sailors. I get to dance a hornpipe."

"When does the play open?" Rosie asked. "Maybe we could come."

Lyle clapped both hands to his head and said, "He's perfect! I should have thought of it instantly. Bone Breath is perfect!"

"Yip!" said Bone Breath.

"Perfect for what?" Kayo said.

"The theater needs a small dog to play a part in this show. All the dogs who auditioned were either too big, or they barked all the time, or their owners weren't available to be backstage for all the rehearsals and performances."

7

"What would Bone Breath have to do?" Rosie asked. "He isn't very well trained."

"He flunked puppy kindergarten," Kayo said.

"He wouldn't have to memorize any lines," Lyle said. "In the play the dog is a pampered pet."

"Bone Breath can do that," said Rosie. "He wouldn't even have to pretend."

Lyle continued. "A wealthy woman takes her dog with her to sail from England to America. The ship is attacked by pirates. The dog appears only twice—three times, if you count the curtain call—and each time the woman carries him." Lyle grinned. "Instead of a walk-on part, the dog's role is a carry-on part."

"It would be fun to see Bone Breath on stage," Rosie said.

Kayo nodded. "He would love all the attention. It could be an extra Care Club project, just for Bone Breath."

"We're on our way to get an ice-cream cone," Rosie said to Lyle. "Why don't you go with us?"

"The producer is looking for people to work backstage," Lyle said as they walked. "Maybe you could help with costumes or props."

After they got their cones, the three kids sat on a shaded bench to eat them. Bone Breath pawed at Rosie's shoes.

"Bone Breath loves ice cream," Rosie said. "If an ice-cream company came out with a line of flavors for dogs, they'd make a billion dollars. They could have Dry Bread Crust and Leftover Spaghetti."

"How about Cat Crunchy?" Kayo suggested. "Bone Breath always tries to get Webster's food."

"Dead Fish," said Lyle. "When we went to the beach, my cousin's dog kept rubbing his face on a dead fish. That night the whole cabin stunk like dead fish. The dog loved it."

"The all-time best-selling ice-cream flavor for dogs would be Garbage Can," Rosie said.

"One scoop of Garbage Can and one scoop of Dead Fish," said Lyle. "How does that sound, Bone Breath?"

Bone Breath wagged his tail and drooled.

They finished their cones, and since *The Oakwood Daily Herald* had not yet arrived at the newsstand and *USA Today* didn't have anything about the forgery on the front page, they started for home. At the far end of the parking lot, they heard a dog barking.

"Oh, no," Rosie said. "Someone left a dog shut in a car."

The three children peered in the windows of a late-model blue sedan which was parked in the sun. A small white dog stood on the front seat. The dog's tongue hung out, his eyes looked frantic, and he panted heavily in between barks.

"It must be boiling hot in there," Lyle said.

9

"That dog needs help," Kayo said.

"All the doors are locked," Rosie said.

"Let's run to the closest stores and try to find the owner," Lyle said.

Rosie wrote the car's license plate number in her notebook. The three kids sprinted to the stores nearest to where the car was parked. Kayo went in a camera shop and the ice-cream store. Lyle went in a shoe store. Rosie carried Bone Breath into a large drugstore, where it took a few minutes to find the manager and explain the problem. The manager immediately paged the car's owner on the store's speaker system.

The kids hurried back to the blue car. The dog pawed frantically at the upholstery, barking a shrill, high bark.

The owner did not come.

Chapter 2

$\mathcal{A}$ car pulled into a parking place two spots over. A gray-haired woman got out, scowling at the children. "What are you kids doing to that car?" she said.

"There's a dog locked inside," Rosie said.

"In this heat?" the woman said. "It's ninety-two degrees outside; I just heard it on the radio."

"We can't find the owner," Lyle said.

The woman looked in the window at the dog. "I'll call the police," she said. She ran back to her car, unlocked it, and grabbed a cellular phone.

"I don't think we can wait for the police," Rosie said. "The dog is foaming at the mouth and his eyes are bulged out."

The dog quit barking. His sides heaved, as if he needed to vomit.

"That dog could die before the police get here," Kayo said.

"We'll have to break in," Lyle said.

Rosie, Kayo, and Lyle looked around for something to use to break the car's window. They saw nothing that would work.

The woman with the car phone said, "The police will come as soon as they can."

"Do you have a jack handle or wrench in your trunk that we can use to break a window?" Kayo asked.

"I am not breaking into someone else's car," the woman said. "That's against the law."

"But the dog is dying!" Kayo said.

"I told the police to hurry," the woman replied.

"If it were my dog in there," Lyle said, "I'd want someone to break my car window."

"If I put my shoe on my hand, to protect myself from broken glass," Rosie said, "I might be able to smash the window." She untied her right sneaker and took it off.

"I'll help," said Kayo as she removed a shoe.

"Me, too," said Lyle. He took off one shoe.

"You'll get arrested," the woman warned. "All three of you."

Rosie handed Bone Breath's leash to the woman.

"Please keep my dog away from the car," Rosie said, "in case the glass falls this way."

"You are asking for trouble," the woman said,

but she took the leash and moved away from the car, staying in the shade formed by a big van.

Rosie, Kayo, and Lyle stood together beside the back window of the car, behind the driver's seat. They each had one hand stuck inside a shoe.

"Now!" cried Rosie.

They hit the window with their shoes, as hard as they could.

Bone Breath barked.

Hairline cracks appeared in the glass, but the window held firm.

"Harder!" Lyle said.

They pounded again, hitting the window over and over until it shattered. Glass flew across the backseat.

A blast of sweltering air came from the broken window, as if they had opened the door of a hot oven.

Rosie reached through the opening and unlocked the front door. Lyle opened it.

As soon as the door was open, Kayo held her closed fist in front of the dog's nose, for him to sniff.

The dog was too sick to notice. Kayo put her hands on the dog's sides.

"His fur is hot," she said. "He feels like a piece of toast."

"There's a veterinary hospital about six blocks from here," the woman said. "If you can get him in my car, I'll take you there."

Kayo carefully lifted the dog out of the car.

The manager of the drugstore ran up, carrying a large glass of water. "I thought the dog might need a drink," she said. She looked at the dog lying limply in Kayo's arms. Then she dumped the glass of water on the dog's head. The dog blinked and shook his head slightly.

A police car pulled into the parking lot and Officer Ken Bremner jumped out.

"You again," Officer Bremner said, when he saw Rosie and Kayo. He looked at the shattered car window. "I hope you didn't break that window," he said.

"We had to," Kayo said. "The dog was dying."

"We can answer questions after we get this dog to a vet," Rosie said.

Officer Bremner looked closely at the little white dog. "Get in," he said. "I'll drive you." He stuck a business card under the windshield wiper of the blue car.

"I'll follow you," said the woman. "I want to know what happens."

With his siren shrieking and his blue lights whirling, Officer Bremner rushed to All Critters Animal Hospital. Kayo handed the dog to Dr. Bishop, who carried the dog to the back of the clinic, put him in a stainless-steel sink, and sprayed cold water on him.

As the veterinarian and his staff worked on the

dog, the three children, Officer Bremner, and the woman who had helped waited in the reception area. Bone Breath waited in the air-conditioned patrol car, because he could tell by the smell that it was a veterinary hospital and he shook with fear until Officer Bremner said Rosie could put him in the car.

Officer Bremner wrote down names and listened to what had happened in the parking lot.

Dr. Bishop came out to report that he was giving the dog fluids intravenously. "Another five minutes," he said, "and it would have been too late. The dog was dying from heatstroke. His eyes were glazed and his heart was racing. Animals should never be left in a car, even with the windows cracked. Temperatures inside soar quickly, causing heatstroke, brain damage, and death. On a day like this, it was probably a hundred and twenty degrees in that car."

Officer Bremner said, "I hope the city prosecutor does not file charges against these kids for breaking into the car."

"The prosecutor should file charges against the dog's owner," Dr. Bishop said, "for cruelty to animals."

"I agree," Officer Bremner said. "Still, the law's the law and breaking into a vehicle is criminal trespassing."

Rosie, Kayo, and Lyle looked at one another nervously.

"The dog has an identification tag," Dr. Bishop said. "I've left a message on the owner's answering machine."

When they knew the dog was going to recover, Officer Bremner drove the children and Bone Breath to Rosie's house. "Have your mother call me," he told Rosie.

"Rosie's mom is a lawyer," Kayo whispered to Lyle.

As the kids climbed out of the patrol car, Mr. Saunders hurried out of the house. Officer Bremner explained what had happened and what charges could be filed.

When Mr. Saunders had heard the whole story, he put a hand on Rosie's shoulder. "You did the right thing," he said.

Rosie let out a sigh of relief.

"For the dog, yes," Officer Bremner said. "Legally, maybe not."

Sammy rode up on his bicycle. "Did you catch the forger already?" Sammy asked.

"We are not trying to catch the forger," Rosie said.

"I am glad to hear that," said Officer Bremner.

"So am I," said Mr. Saunders.

Officer Bremner left and Mr. Saunders went inside.

Lyle said, "If I get arrested for criminal trespassing, my parents will have a fit."

"You guys were trespassing?" Sammy said. "Where? In the forger's house?"

Lyle explained what had happened.

Sammy said, "You should have put mustard and catsup on the hot dog." He laughed and slapped his handlebars.

Nobody else smiled.

"Don't you get it?" Sammy said. "Put mustard and—"

"We got it," Rosie said.

"I have to go home," Lyle said. "I told my mom I'd only be gone an hour."

After Lyle left, the girls went inside and found *The Oakwood Daily Herald* next to Mr. Saunders's favorite chair.

Kayo usually read the sports section first, while Rosie worked the crossword puzzle. That day both girls read every word of the front-page article.

ART MUSEUM'S VAN GOGH DECLARED A FORGERY

The Oakwood Art Museum's most valuable painting, believed to be an original by Vincent Van Gogh, was labeled today as a forgery. *Two Cut Sunflowers* was recently donated to the museum as part of the estate of the late Truman Handel, founder of Handel Computers.

According to the Handel family, the painting was purchased two years ago at an auction for $1.3 million. It had a certificate of authenticity from Dr. Claude Montfort, a highly respected art historian in Paris. Dr. Montfort could not be reached for comment.

Museum director Sharon Hulit said the museum always has any painting valued at more than $100,000 checked by its own authorities to verify its value for insurance purposes. When lab tests were done on *Two Cut Sunflowers*, infrared rays showed false crackle; the painting looks old, but it is not. "This was the most important painting our museum owned," Miss Hulit said. "It's an incredibly skillful forgery; all of us are shocked."

Anyone with information should contact the Oakwood Police.

"It doesn't sound likely that they'll catch the forger," Rosie said. "Not if the painting was purchased two years ago."

"Right now," Kayo said, "I'm more worried about the owner of the car we broke into."

Chapter 3

"Did you get arrested?" Sammy asked when Rosie and Kayo got to school the next morning.

"Strike one," said Kayo.

"No," said Rosie.

Sammy looked disappointed. "If you go to jail," he said, "I'll visit you. You can tell me all the details of what you did, and I'll write them down and sell the story to a TV station or a magazine."

"Strike two," said Kayo.

"What a despicable idea," said Rosie. She made a check in her notebook.

"Is that good or bad?" asked Sammy.

"Despicable," said Rosie, "means it's so unworthy and obnoxious that it should be despised."

"A dirty, rotten scumbag of an idea," added Kayo.

Lyle joined them. "The dog we rescued was on the TV news last night," he said. "The veterinarian told how the dog nearly died."

"I saw it," Kayo said.

"Mom talked with the city prosecutor," Rosie said. "The city is not going to press charges against us."

"Rats," said Sammy.

"Strike three," said Kayo. She and Rosie walked to their desks and sat down.

Lyle followed them.

"I don't care if I can't sell your story," Sammy said. "By this time next week I'll have my five thousand dollars." He plopped into his own seat, in the back row.

Rosie lowered her voice so only Kayo and Lyle could hear her. "The man who owns the dog has been charged with animal cruelty," she said, "and he is furious about it. He says he's going to sue all of us."

Kayo removed her Cleveland Indians baseball cap, smoothed back her hair, and put the cap in her backpack. "If he wins a lawsuit against me," she said, "Mom and I could never pay him. It's a struggle to pay the rent and the electric bill."

"He won't win," Rosie said. "My dad says it will be a cold day in you-know-where before any judge or jury awards damages to someone who locks his dog in a car on a sweltering hot day."

"I hope he's right," Kayo said.

"Did you ask your parents if Bone Breath can be in the play?" Lyle said.

"Dad called the director," Rosie said. "Bone Breath is going to audition tonight before the rehearsal. My parents said as long as I don't get behind in my homework, I can stay at the theater with Bone Breath every night."

"If he gets the part, I can help backstage, too," Kayo said.

"Our parents agreed to carpool," Rosie added.

"Could we make it a three-way carpool?" Lyle asked. "My parents are not thrilled about driving me to and from the theater every night."

"That would be great," Rosie said, "as long as you don't mind a little dog fur in the car."

That evening Mr. Saunders drove Rosie, Kayo, Lyle, and the freshly shampooed Bone Breath to the Oakwood Community Theater. The theater was in an old warehouse beside some unused railroad tracks. Part of the building was an art gallery and shop; the largest part was the theater. A lighted sign over the theater door said OPENING SOON: PIRATE'S PLUNDER.

"Maybe Bone Breath will have his name up in lights," Rosie said.

Mr. Saunders frowned at the abandoned house across the street from the theater, and at the sign

21

on the vacant lot on the corner that said WILL BUILD TO SUIT. The lettering on the sign was faded from months of rain and sun.

"This isn't exactly the high-rent district," Mr. Saunders said. "I don't want you to leave the theater building."

"We won't," Rosie said, looking up and down the street. "There's no place to go."

The director of the play, Mrs. Posh, took one look at Bone Breath and said, "It's Daisy!"

"Who?" said Kayo.

"That's the dog's name in the play," Lyle explained.

"She's perfect," Mrs. Posh said.

"It's a he," Rosie said.

"Who can tell, with all that shaggy fur?" said Mrs. Posh. She patted Bone Breath on the head. "Good Daisy," she said. "Nice dog. You want to be in the play, don't you, Daisy?"

Bone Breath wagged his tail and licked the director's hand.

"Oooh," squealed a red-haired woman as she rushed onto the stage. "Is this going to be my little doggie sweetums?" She put her face in front of Bone Breath's face. "You are sooo cuuute!" she cried. "You are my itty-bitty furry sweetheart!"

Bone Breath wriggled with delight.

Rosie glanced at Kayo, who was trying not to laugh.

"Daisy," said Mrs. Posh, "meet your stage mother."

Bone Breath licked the woman on the lips.

"You're getting dog germs, Carmen," said Mrs. Posh.

"There are fewer germs in a dog's mouth than in a human's," Lyle said.

"I'd rather kiss a dog than a man, any day," said Carmen.

The kids laughed. Mrs. Posh rolled her eyes toward the ceiling.

"Come to Carmen, darling Daisy," Carmen said, holding out her arms.

Bone Breath leaped happily out of Rosie's arms and snuggled against the woman's ample chest. Carmen laid her cheek on Bone Breath's head as she petted him and talked baby talk to him.

"One of you kids will need to stay with Daisy at all times when she isn't onstage," Mrs. Posh said.

"We will," Rosie promised.

"And take her for a walk before you bring her in here."

"We walked him just before we left home," Rosie said.

"Then it's settled," said Mrs. Posh. "Your dog has the role of Daisy, and you girls are the props crew." She handed Kayo two play scripts and a piece of paper. "Here's a script for each of you, and a list of the props we still need. Beg and borrow as much as you can; we have a limited budget. And bring them as soon as possible."

"We will," Kayo said.

"We're keeping everything for this production in the front of the storage room, until the set is ready. There's a master list of props on the wall. Be sure to cross off anything you bring, so others will quit hunting for it." She smiled. "You'll be glad to know we already have a cannon."

Carmen gave Bone Breath back to Rosie. "I'll pick her up in the green room before we go on each time," she said.

"Him," Rosie said.

Carmen puckered up her lips and made kissing noises in front of Bone Breath's nose. "Be my good little baby sweetums till I come to get you," she said before she headed across the stage.

Rosie snapped the leash on Bone Breath and led him down the steps into the auditorium, where Mr. Saunders sat.

"Great audition, Bone Breath," Lyle said. "Welcome to the show."

Mr. Saunders said, "I'll be back at ten to drive you and Itty Bitty Sweetums home."

"He probably won't want to go home," Rosie said. "He'll want to move in with Carmen."

"This is going to be a fun Care Club project," Kayo said.

Backstage Fright

The smile faded from Mr. Saunders's face. "This is a Care Club project?" he said. "Maybe I should stick around, just in case."

"In case what?" Lyle asked.

"My dad has this silly idea that every time our club does a project, we end up in danger," Rosie said.

"We do," Kayo said.

"The whole cast of *Pirate's Plunder* is here," Rosie said, "plus the stage manager and Mrs. Posh. With so many people around, we will be perfectly safe."

"Where have I heard this before?" Mr. Saunders said, but he left the theater and drove home.

Chapter 4

Lyle introduced Kayo and Rosie to the actors: Charlie, Dave, Norm, Eddie, and Dean. Carmen was the only woman; the rest of the cast played the roles of sailors or pirates. Everyone smiled, welcomed the girls, and petted Bone Breath.

Lyle showed the girls the stage manager's station, pointed out the bathrooms, and walked through the construction area where scenery was built and painted.

"Where is the green room?" Rosie asked. "That's where Carmen said she would come for Bone Breath."

"Right here," Lyle said, opening a door. The small room contained a drab brown sofa with stuffing coming out of one seat cushion, three beat-up but comfortable-looking gray chairs, a small refrigerator, a coffeepot, and a table littered with mugs, paper napkins, a stack of scripts from former plays, a cottage cheese carton containing an inch of nickels, dimes, and quarters, and a half-full box of chocolate-covered doughnuts. "This is where the actors wait when they aren't onstage."

"The walls are yellow," Rosie said, "not green."

"Every theater has a room where the actors wait," Lyle explained, "and it's always called the green room, no matter what color it is."

Bone Breath sniffed the floor under the table and licked up a few doughnut crumbs.

"There are soft drinks in the fridge," Lyle said. "Help yourself and put your money in the cup." He pointed to the cottage cheese carton. "Food is free," he added as he took a doughnut.

The girls each took one, too. While they ate, Kayo read aloud the list of props they were supposed to find.

PROP LIST FOR "PIRATE'S PLUNDER"

1. Jolly Roger (black flag with skull and crossbones on it)
2. Human skeleton
3. Four swords
4. Two leg-irons (ball and chain)

5. Six tin cups
6. Figurehead from old sailing ship
7. Two pistols with long barrels
8. Long-handled spade
9. Old chest with leather straps
10. Bags of gold coins
11. Plain red flag
12. Old-looking treasure map
13. Coil of rope

"How will we ever find such weird things?" Kayo said. "We can't walk into a store and ask to borrow leg-irons. I don't even know what they are."

"It's a thick chain attached to an iron ball," Lyle said. "A clamp goes around the prisoner's ankle. The prisoner can't run away, because the ball and chain are too heavy."

"Maybe we could get a couple of black bowling balls," Rosie said, "and attach some heavy chains to them."

"When we offered to get props," Kayo said, "I thought it would be easy. This list is impossible."

"Let's begin by looking in the storage room," Lyle suggested. "Props are stored in there from every play the group has ever done. Nothing gets thrown out, because it might be needed again."

He led the way to the far back of the building and opened a door.

Wooden shelves climbed the walls of the large storage room, and freestanding metal shelves formed narrow aisles. The shelves overflowed with dishes, books, fake food, medical equipment, a stuffed owl, plastic flowers, and other items. Costumes hung from rolling racks. A fake fireplace, a statue of a mermaid, a huge plastic palm tree, an ugly purple urn, and a wicker baby buggy clogged one aisle. A large cannon sat near the door.

"There is so much junk in here," Kayo said, "the play will be over before we can look at it all."

"We can go through it quickly since we have specific things to look for," Rosie said.

Kayo sneezed. "This room has not been dusted in years," she said.

"Correction," said Lyle. "This room has not been dusted, ever."

Rosie shut the door behind them and let Bone Breath off the leash. Bone Breath sniffed the hems of the costumes, the dishes on the bottom shelves, and a set of wooden chairs. His tail wagged as he moved rapidly around the room, clearly excited.

"People go sight-seeing in a new place," Rosie said. "Dogs go sight-smelling."

"That's because of the two hundred and twenty million cells in his nose," Lyle said.

"Hey!" Rosie said as she dug through the contents of a big cardboard box. "I found some tin cups."

"Are there six of them?" Kayo asked.

"There are eight."

"Hooray!" said Kayo. "We can cross *tin cups* off the prop list. Now we need to find a skeleton."

"Maybe we could use this mermaid statue as the figurehead," Rosie said.

A heavy green curtain hung along the back wall of the storage room, its two sides overlapping in the center. Bone Breath stuck his head under the curtain, and then disappeared behind it.

"Bone Breath," Rosie said. "Come back here where I can see you."

Bone Breath did not come.

Rosie pushed her way between the overlapping sections of the curtain. Dust billowed into the air when she moved the heavy fabric.

Kayo sneezed again.

Rosie covered her nose and mouth with her hand. "There's space back here," Rosie said, "between the curtain and the wall. It's like a narrow hallway."

"Are there any skeletons?" Kayo asked.

"No. Only some old paintings and a door." She tried the knob. "It's locked from the other side."

"If there isn't a skeleton, an old chest, or something else from our list," Kayo said, "don't waste your time back there." She dug through the contents of another cardboard box.

"I'm going back to the rehearsal," Lyle said. "I'm on soon."

"Come and get us when your part is finished," Kayo said, "so we can have Bone Breath ready on time."

Lyle left.

"Kayo!" Rosie's voice from behind the green curtain was tense. "Come here."

Kayo poked her head between the halves of the curtain, holding her nose. "What do you want?"

"Come back here. Look what I found."

Kayo went behind the curtain.

Rosie held a framed oil painting. As Kayo approached, Rosie turned the painting around so Kayo could see it.

Kayo immediately recognized the blue background with the bright yellow and gold sunflowers. *Two Cut Sunflowers* by Vincent Van Gogh.

Chapter 5

How did the museum's painting get here?" Kayo said.

"This isn't the museum's painting," Rosie replied. "Their picture was never stolen. But this might be another forgery, or maybe it's the original Van Gogh."

Rosie held the painting carefully, touching only the frame. If it was a genuine Van Gogh, it was painted in the late 1880s. Rosie wasn't going to put fingerprints on a work of art that was over one hundred years old and worth more than a million dollars.

Rosie remembered what Mrs. Cushman had said about the Dutch artist before the class went to the art museum. Vincent Van Gogh was often depressed and had bouts of insanity for which he was hospitalized. He sold only one painting during his lifetime, a fact which Rosie found terribly sad. If his talent had been recognized while he was living, he might have been happier.

Kayo squinted at the painting. Not much light from the storage room came over the top of the heavy curtain. "Maybe this is only a print," she said. "Mrs. Cushman said there are lots of prints made of famous paintings. They take a picture of the real painting and make prints from the negative, the same way we get extra prints of pictures we take with a camera."

Rosie held the painting at eye level and looked across the surface. "The surface is rough," she said. "I think a print would be smooth."

"What are the other paintings?" Kayo asked, pointing toward two more framed pictures.

"An old barn and a bowl of fruit. Nothing unusual. This one was facing the wall and the others were in front of it."

"Since this is the painting that has the museum in such an uproar," Kayo said, "I think we should tell Mrs. Posh what we found."

"I agree," Rosie said as she put the painting back where she had found it. She leashed Bone Breath, and the girls hurried out to the rehearsal.

At the next break Rosie and Kayo approached the director.

"We found some framed paintings in the storage room," Rosie said.

"There are dozens of paintings in the storage room," Mrs. Posh said.

"One of them is *Two Cut Sunflowers* by Vincent Van Gogh," Kayo said. "That's the painting that the art museum thought was an original, only it turned out they have a forgery. We found it way in back, behind the green curtain."

"Anything behind that curtain has been there for at least ten years," Mrs. Posh said. "That's how long ago we got our new curtain, and we hung the old one in the storage room as soon as the new one was in place. I doubt if anyone has gone behind it since. Those paintings should be moved out from behind the curtain where they'll be seen by anyone looking for pictures to decorate a set."

"Then you don't think the painting we found could be valuable?" Rosie asked.

"Goodness, no," Mrs. Posh said. "If it's in that storage room, it was donated as a prop for a play."

One of the actors walked up with a question for Mrs. Posh. When she turned her attention to him, the girls left the stage. Kayo said, "Let's go move the paintings out from behind the curtain."

As they walked back to the storage room, Rosie said, "I'm glad the painting is just an old prop.

For once, I want to enjoy our Care Club project and not get pulled into a mystery."

They entered the storage room and went behind the green curtain. This time Rosie kept Bone Breath on his leash. Kayo picked up the two other paintings. Rosie picked up *Two Cut Sunflowers*.

Kayo pushed through the curtain and walked to the middle of the room.

Rosie stayed behind in the narrow corridor.

"Are you coming?" Kayo asked.

"No," Rosie said.

Her voice sounded odd. Kayo pushed her way through the curtain again, muffling a sneeze.

"What's the matter?" Kayo asked when she saw Rosie still standing in the small corridor.

"I didn't want to get my new shirt dirty," Rosie said, "so I ran my hand along the top of the frame before I picked the painting up." She held her hand out toward Kayo. "There wasn't any dust on it."

Kayo dragged her right hand across the top of one of the frames she carried. A thick layer of dust clung to her fingers. She ran her left hand across the top of the other picture frame with the same result. She said, "Both of these are filthy."

"This one has no dust at all," Rosie said. "It has not been here more than a few days."

"Maybe we shouldn't move these," Kayo said.

"Mrs. Posh doesn't think anyone comes back here, but she must be wrong."

They carefully replaced the paintings where they had originally been. "It bothers me that *Two Cut Sunflowers* is the one that isn't dusty," Rosie said. "Even though Mrs. Posh says it's only an old prop, it *is* the painting that's caused trouble for the museum."

"Let's report this to the police," Kayo said. "Mom says it's better to call the police and have it turn out to be unnecessary, than not to call them and wish you had."

"I saw a phone in the green room; we can call from there."

The police officer who took the call said, "It's probably a worthless print, but we'll check into it." He thanked Rosie for calling and hung up.

"He didn't even ask for my phone number," Rosie said.

"Good," Kayo said. "I really don't want to get involved with the police again."

"We reported it," Rosie said, "so now let's forget it and enjoy helping with the play."

They took Bone Breath into the auditorium and sat down to watch the rest of the rehearsal.

The next night the kids arrived at the theater with their arms full of props.

Mr. Saunders had loaned them a long-handled

spade. "I'll draw the treasure map for you, too," he said. "Give me a day or two to find the right kind of paper."

Rosie's father was a professional cartoonist; she knew the treasure map would be exactly what Mrs. Posh wanted. "Thanks, Dad," she said as she gave him a hug.

Mrs. Saunders had astonished Rosie by going into the attic and returning with two swords.

"They belonged to my great-grandfather," she said. "I've never liked seeing weapons displayed in a house, but I didn't want to get rid of them, either, so I've kept them packed away."

"They're perfect," Rosie said, and she hugged her mother, too.

Mrs. Benton helped Kayo make a red flag out of material left from a holiday sewing project. Lyle's parents contributed a large coil of rope and a bag of chocolate coins wrapped in gold foil.

"When the play is over, we can eat them," Lyle said.

"Maybe this isn't going to be as hard as we thought," Kayo said as Mr. Saunders helped them unload everything from the trunk of his car.

They went straight to the storage room to leave their props. Kayo found the master list of props and crossed off *spade, red flag, treasure map,* and *rope.* As she was changing *four swords* to *two swords,* Rosie said, "I wonder if the police ever came and looked at the painting we found."

"I want to see it," Lyle said. "I hadn't moved to Oakwood yet when the sixth grade toured the art museum, so I don't know what the painting by Vincent Van Gogh looks like."

The three children and Bone Breath crowded into the narrow space behind the green curtain. Bone Breath sniffed the locked door. Kayo held up *Two Cut Sunflowers* for Lyle to see.

"No wonder Van Gogh is famous," Lyle said.

"He did a painting of sunflowers in a vase that I like even better than this one," Rosie said.

The kids heard a *click* as the door to the storage room opened.

"Hello," Kayo called.

There was no answer.

"We're back here, behind the curtain," Kayo added, thinking whoever had come in was looking for them.

"Get out of there." The man's voice was low, but he sounded angry.

Bone Breath growled. Rosie gripped the leash tightly and said, "Shh."

Kayo put the painting down.

"Don't go back there again," the voice said.

Rosie scowled indignantly at the curtain, as if she could see through it. Who was this man, and what right did he have to boss them around? Why did he care if they went behind the curtain?

Staying close together, the three kids pushed through the opening in the curtain.

"What's the trouble?" Lyle said as they stepped back into the storage room.

Nobody answered.

The kids looked quickly around.

No one was there. The man who had spoken to them had left, shutting the door behind him.

Kayo ran to the door and opened it. Down the hall, in front of the green room, several actors stood together, talking and laughing. Nothing seemed unusual.

"Did you recognize the voice?" Rosie asked Lyle.

He shook his head. "It sounded like a threat when he told us not to go back there again."

"I don't like this," said Rosie.

"Neither do I," said Kayo.

"What shall we do about it?" Lyle asked. "Tell Mrs. Posh?"

"We aren't going to do anything about it," said Rosie.

Lyle's eyebrows went up in surprise.

"We've already told the police what we found," Rosie said, "and that's all we're going to do."

"She's right," Kayo said. "If whoever spoke to

us wants us to stay out of that back area, then we'll stay out. Why ask for problems?"

"But what if it isn't an old prop?" Lyle said. "What if it's another forgery and someone plans to pass it off as the original? Somebody could end up spending a million dollars for it, just like Mr. Handel did."

Rosie frowned.

Kayo sighed.

"I suppose we should try to find out if the painting is valuable or not," Rosie said.

"There's an art gallery next to the theater," Kayo said. "Let's take the painting over there, and ask if it has any value. If it is an inexpensive copy, we'll return it and forget it. If it isn't . . ." Her voice trailed away.

She really didn't want to think about what they might have to do if the painting was not a discarded prop.

Chapter 6

If the painting is valuable, we'll call the police again," Rosie said. "Even better, we'll tell our parents and let them call the police."

"We can't do it now," Lyle said. "It's time for rehearsal to start."

"I don't want anyone to see us with the painting," Kayo said. "We don't know who told us to stay away, but if he saw us with the painting, he'd know we didn't do what he said."

"Let's come to rehearsal early tomorrow," Lyle suggested. "We can take the painting next door, show it to someone at the gallery, and return it before the rest of the cast and crew arrive."

"Won't the theater be locked, if no one is here?" Kayo said.

"There's a key hidden around in back," Lyle

said. "Mrs. Posh told us about it at the first rehearsal."

Lyle glanced at his watch. "We'd better get out there. Mrs. Posh always starts on time."

The kids found seats in the front row. A few other cast members sat there, too, but most stood around onstage.

"We have a replacement pirate," Mrs. Posh said. "This is Chip Stanford and he's taking over for Charlie, who got called out of town on a family emergency."

Chip waved a hand in greeting.

"I have one question," Dean said. "Are you married, Chip?"

"Yes," he said.

"Too bad, Carmen," said Dean.

"Carmen prefers dog kisses, anyway," said Norm.

"We're going to take it from the top tonight," Mrs. Posh said. "Act One, Scene One. Let's go."

Carmen, with a purple and gold scarf flung across her shoulders, swooped off the stage toward Bone Breath. "There's my sweet baby darlin'," she said. "Carmen missed you, little love."

Bone Breath's whole body trembled with pleasure. Carmen reached for him, and Bone Breath gladly cuddled against her as Carmen buried her face in his fur and murmured, "Oh, you are just the dearest little thing I've ever seen."

The girls watched while Carmen carried Bone Breath onstage. When she changed from her baby-talk voice to her actress voice and began speaking her lines, Bone Breath cocked his head to one side and looked at her, as if wondering why she was speaking in a strange way. But he never tried to jump out of her arms and he paid no attention to the other actors. He just gazed lovingly at Carmen until his scene was over and he was carried back to Rosie.

"This dog is one fine little actress," Carmen said.

"Actor," Rosie corrected.

Instead of watching the rehearsal, Rosie and Kayo went into the green room to do their homework.

"I can't concentrate," Kayo said. "I keep wondering who told us to stay away from those paintings."

"And why," Rosie said.

The next day Rosie, Kayo, Lyle, and Bone Breath arrived at the theater an hour early.

Lyle led the way around the side of the building. He walked to a raised wooden platform that held three garbage cans.

When Bone Breath saw the garbage cans, he tugged forward eagerly and began sniffing around the bottom of the platform.

"Bone Breath thinks it's a restaurant for dogs," Rosie said.

Lyle picked up a large rock from the ground beside the platform; the theater key was under the rock.

They went back to the front of the theater and unlocked the door. Kayo waved to her mother, who had waited to be sure the children got safely inside, and Mrs. Benton drove off.

Lyle replaced the key while Kayo and Rosie went to the storage room, walked behind the green curtain, and removed the painting of *Two Cut Sunflowers*. They carried it to the theater lobby and met Lyle there.

"Let's hurry," Kayo said. "I want to put this back before anyone else gets here." She held the painting across her chest with the front toward her shirt.

A small brass bell jingled on the door of the art gallery when they entered. They were greeted by a woman wearing a name badge that said MARTHA. Eyeglasses hung from a chain around her neck. She leaned on a metal walker as she moved slowly toward them, with hunched shoulders. Her hip purse looked out of place with her old-fashioned flowered dress and sensible laced shoes.

"Is it all right if I bring my dog inside?" Rosie asked.

"As long as you keep him under control," Martha said. "I'm not very steady on my feet anymore."

A white-haired woman rose from a chair behind a large counter. A fringed shawl, draped around her shoulders, was held in place with a brooch. Her name badge said HELEN.

"That's the biggest painting I ever saw," Lyle said, pointing to an unframed canvas on the back wall that was eight feet high by five feet wide, covered with bright splashes of red, green, and yellow. He wanted to ask what it was supposed to be, but he was afraid he might offend the owners of the gallery.

"It's called *Stop Light*," said Helen.

Kayo carefully laid *Two Cut Sunflowers* on the countertop.

"Saints alive!" said Helen.

"Wherever did you get that, dear?" asked Martha.

"We found it in the theater's storage room," Kayo said. "We know it's *Two Cut Sunflowers*, and we've read about the trouble with that painting at the art museum."

"What we don't know," Rosie said, "is whether this might be a clue to the police. Is this another forgery? Is it old? Is it valuable?"

As the girls spoke, Martha pushed her walker

close to the counter. Helen opened a drawer and removed a large magnifying glass.

Martha put her glasses on and both women leaned over the painting without touching it, studying it carefully. Then Helen picked it up by the frame and turned it over. They looked just as carefully at the back side.

"Why do you look at the back of it?" Rosie asked.

"There might be old stamps on the back," Helen said, "or inscriptions."

They turned the painting faceup again.

"It looks old," Lyle said. "It's all crackled."

"There are ways to do that," Martha said. "A good forger can age a painting four hundred years."

"This is definitely not an authentic Van Gogh," Helen said. "I've seen original Van Gogh paintings at the Museum of Modern Art in New York City. This lacks the intense coloration."

"I agree," Martha said. "This is a decent copy, but nothing special."

"So this painting won't help the police or the art museum?" Lyle said.

"No," Martha said.

"And it isn't worth a lot of money?" Rosie said.

"I'm afraid not," Helen said.

Kayo blew out her breath in relief. "Good," she said.

"Most people are disappointed when we tell them that the painting they brought in is not valuable," Martha said.

"Now we can put it back where we found it," Kayo said, "and forget about it. If it had been valuable, or of some use to the police, we would have had to turn it in, and then the man who told us to stay away from it would be angry."

"Saints alive!" Helen said.

Martha stiffened, clutching her walker. "What man?" she said.

Kayo explained.

The two women seemed upset. "Don't go in the storage area again," Helen urged. "It sounds as if there's another crazy actor in that theater group. You children could be in danger."

"There are angry fools everywhere these days," Martha said, "and many of them carry weapons. It isn't safe to cross them."

Helen put the magnifying glass back in the drawer.

Martha took off her glasses and let them drop to her chest.

Kayo picked up the painting and turned to leave.

"There is a door behind the curtain where the painting was," Rosie said. "From the layout of the theater, that door should open into the back of your gallery." She pointed to the back wall as she spoke. "But there isn't any door on this side."

Martha said, "Don't go near that door, dear, whatever you do."

"Stay away from that door," Helen agreed. "We had it boarded over on this side years ago, right after the murder."

Chapter
7

"What murder?" Kayo asked.

"Oh, it was terrible, dear," Martha said. "Two actors argued and one picked up a knife that was a prop in a play and chased the second man into the storage room and stabbed him."

"How despicable," Rosie said.

"Then the murderer opened that door," Martha continued, "ran through our gallery, and disappeared into the night. He was never caught."

"We found a trail of blood on our floor the next morning," Helen said. "It was horrible. As soon as it was cleaned up, we had the door boarded over and a new wall put up." She leaned toward the children and lowered her voice. "There are bad vibrations in the air in any place where a person has been murdered," she said. "They soak into your skin and make terrible things happen to you."

Martha nodded her head solemnly. "We didn't want those bad vibrations coming into our gallery," she said. "You stay away from that storage room. If you don't, the bad vibrations will soak into you." She looked down at Bone Breath. "And into your little dog, too," she added.

Rosie shuddered. The kindly-looking old woman sounded menacing.

"It isn't just the door," Helen said. "It's the floor all around it, as well."

"Maybe that's why the curtain is hung where it is," Lyle said. "To keep people from going where the murder happened."

"We have to put the painting back," Kayo said.

"You shouldn't do that," Martha said.

"It's an old prop that will never be missed," Helen said. "You can leave it here, if you like, and we'll dispose of it for you."

"If it weren't for the man who warned us to stay away," Rosie said, "we wouldn't return the painting. But if he discovers that it's missing, he'll assume we took it."

"We want to stay out of trouble," Kayo said.

"Don't tell anyone about this," Martha said. "Not even your parents. Put the painting back, if you must, but then stay away from the murder scene. If you don't go there again, the man will probably leave you alone."

"Perhaps it wasn't a man at all," Helen said. "Perhaps it was the ghost of the murdered actor."

The kids looked at one another in stunned silence.

"It's past six-thirty," Kayo said. "We need to get back over there before anyone else comes."

"Thanks for all your help," Rosie said.

"Anytime," Martha replied. Pushing her walker and taking slow, deliberate steps, she followed the children to the door. "Be careful," she said.

"Be careful," echoed Helen. "Remember the bad vibrations."

The three friends hurried into the theater and down the aisle toward the stage. They climbed the steps on the side of the stage and went behind the stage manager's station.

Just then they heard voices ahead of them. A hammer pounded. A power saw buzzed.

The kids stopped walking.

"The crew is working on the set," Kayo said. "We have to walk past them to get to the storage room."

"They can only work until rehearsal starts," Lyle said, "because they make too much noise."

"We'll have to sneak the painting into the storage room later," Rosie said.

They looked in the green room and were relieved to find the room empty. Kayo quickly stuck the painting under the sofa cushion. Rosie and Lyle sat on the cushion while Kayo paced nervously around the room. Bone Breath sniffed hopefully under the table, searching for crumbs.

Dave came in and started the coffeepot. He wore a fake beard and had a jagged scar on one cheek. "Don't forget," he said to Lyle, "we're supposed to be in costume tonight."

Dean, wearing an old naval uniform, brought a plate of brownies in and set it on the table. "Help yourself," he said.

Kayo took a brownie.

Carmen, in a long brown coat and a hat with a huge feather on it, swept in and descended on Bone Breath. "Here's your costume, Lovey-dovey," she said as she tied a huge pink bow to his collar.

Bone Breath turned his head sideways and tried to bite the bow. Carmen reached into her oversize handbag and brought out a dog biscuit. That, and more baby talk, distracted him.

Twice Rosie bent forward and looked to be sure the painting wasn't sticking out from under the sofa cushion. She didn't want to have to answer any questions.

Several other cast and crew members came in to get coffee or soft drinks. The brownies disappeared quickly. The actors looked so different in their costumes, especially the pirates.

"You look scary," Rosie told Dave.

"Good," he replied. "I'm supposed to be a murderer."

"Were any of you in the play here when the actor was really murdered?" Lyle asked.

The buzz of conversation stopped and all eyes turned toward Lyle.

"What play?" asked Dave.

"What murder?" asked Norm.

"I heard that a few years back two actors had a fight, and one of them stabbed the other one with a knife," Lyle said.

"Onstage?" asked Dean.

"In the storage room," Lyle said. "He was never caught."

"That's news to me," said Dave.

"Me, too," said Norm, "and I've been on the board of trustees from the beginning. Who told you there was a murder here?"

Rosie and Kayo both held their breath, hoping Lyle would not mention their visit to the art gallery.

"Oh, just someone I talked to," Lyle said. "I don't even know her last name."

"Your friend was pulling your leg with that story," Dean said. "The only murders in this theater have been pretend ones."

"I need to get my costume on," Lyle said.

"Come back and show us how you look," Rosie said. "I'll stay here." She said *I'll stay here* slowly, so Lyle would know she would not move from the sofa cushion that covered the painting.

Lyle nodded and left the green room, returning a couple of minutes later in a black and white striped T-shirt, black pants that ended tightly just below the knee, and long red stockings.

Mrs. Posh shouted, "Places, everyone!" and all the actors trooped out, leaving Rosie, Kayo, and Lyle alone.

"I have about eight minutes before my entrance," Lyle said. "Let's get rid of the painting."

Kayo opened the door and peeked into the hallway.

"Is anyone out there?" Rosie whispered. "Has the set crew left?"

"I don't see anyone."

Rosie jumped up, lifted the sofa cushion, and removed the painting. Since she had Bone Breath's leash, she handed the painting to Kayo, who tucked it carefully under one arm.

Rosie and Lyle went out the door of the green room, followed by Kayo.

Bone Breath's toenails clicked on the hardwood floor, and Rosie made a mental note to have his nails trimmed.

They passed the set construction area. Kayo

looked back over her shoulder; the hallway was empty.

Rosie swallowed hard.

Lyle quietly turned the doorknob and pushed the storage room door open.

They stepped into the room.

As Kayo entered, she looked at the wall to her left, feeling for the light switch. Just as her fingers found it, Lyle's hand pressed on hers, stopping her from flicking the switch.

Kayo turned toward Lyle, and saw what Lyle and Rosie had already noticed. A faint light shone out from under the green curtain.

Someone was back there.

Chapter
8

Rosie's heart raced; she hoped Bone Breath would not growl or bark. At home Bone Breath barked at anything unusual. He raised a terrible ruckus when the meter reader came to read the electric meter, and he went half crazy if he saw a squirrel in the yard.

Don't bark, Rosie thought. *Please don't bark.* She leaned down and stroked Bone Breath's head, willing him to be quiet.

Silently the kids backed out of the storage room. Kayo clutched the painting to her chest. Lyle pulled the door shut.

No one spoke as they hurried back toward the green room.

They saw Carmen coming toward them. Kayo quickly stepped toward the set construction area, where blue plastic tarps protected the floor from paint. Kayo dropped to one knee, lifted a corner of a tarp, and slid the painting under it. She pretended to tie her shoelace.

Lyle and Rosie walked on, trying to look as if nothing unusual was happening.

"There you are!" Carmen said. "We're skipping ahead to Act Two, Scene Two, so I need my furry little partner."

Bone Breath wagged his tail and slurped Rosie's shoe as she handed the leash to Carmen.

"You are my sweetums, dear Daisy," Carmen said as she turned and led him away.

Kayo watched Carmen leave. She moved farther into the set construction area, out of the hall light. She chose a spot where she could see the storage room door.

With the set crew gone, the lights in the construction area were off. In the dim light from the hallway, the partially built set had an eerie look. Half a stairway ended abruptly in midair. A wall with empty spaces where two windows and a door would go seemed to leer like an oversize jack-o'-lantern.

Kayo stood in the shadows and stared at the door of the storage room. She intended to stay right there until whoever was inside came out, and she could see who it was.

As soon as Carmen and Bone Breath were out

of sight, Rosie and Lyle returned to the set construction area, too.

No one spoke for several minutes. They just stood quietly and watched the storage room door.

No one came out.

"I'm going to open the door," Lyle whispered, "flip on the light switch, and run. If I leave the door open, whoever is in there will come to close it and we can get a look at him."

"I'll come with you," Rosie said. "I can reach in and turn on the light while you push the door open."

Kayo waited near the painting, watching Lyle and Rosie sneak forward. When they reached the door, they stopped and looked at each other. Rosie gave a slight nod.

Lyle turned the doorknob and eased the door open. As soon as the opening was wide enough for her arm to fit through it, Rosie put her hand inside and felt along the wall for the light switch. When she flicked it on, Lyle shoved the door all the way open.

Rosie withdrew her hand and ducked to one side of the door. Lyle turned and ran back to Kayo.

Nothing happened. There was no sound from inside the storage room. After waiting more than a minute, Rosie cautiously peeked inside. The room appeared to be empty.

She turned the light off. This time it was as dark behind the green curtain as it was in the rest of the room. Was someone back there, waiting in the dark?

Kayo picked up the painting. She and Lyle tiptoed down the hallway toward Rosie. They all entered the storage room together, turned the light on, and silently made their way past the shelves and costume racks until they stood where the two sides of the green curtain met in the center.

Once more, Lyle and Rosie looked at each other. Then they each grabbed one half of the curtain and pulled, making an opening big enough to look through. Tiny particles of dust thickened the air. Kayo sneezed.

All three kids pushed through the opening at the same time. They stopped in the narrow space and looked both ways. It was empty.

Kayo put *Two Cut Sunflowers* back where it had been.

Lyle tried to open the door that Martha and Helen had warned him not to touch. The knob didn't turn.

They went back through the curtain and searched the storage room. They looked behind the costume racks and on all sides of the free-standing shelves. Convinced they were the only ones in the storage room, they left.

59

They went as far as the construction area and then stepped into the shadows to talk.

"No one came out of that room, after we saw the light," Kayo said.

"If anyone had come out, they would have had to walk this way," Lyle said.

"No one came out, and no one is in there now," Rosie said, "so who was carrying the light we saw earlier?"

"Maybe there *is* a ghost," Kayo said. "Maybe Martha and Helen told the truth about a murder but they were mixed up about when it happened. People sometimes forget details of past events. Maybe the murder took place before there was a theater in the building."

"That makes sense," Lyle said. "There's no reason for Martha and Helen to lie to us about a murder."

"Maybe it was the ghost who told us to stay away," Kayo said.

"If I heard the voice again, I would recognize it," Rosie said.

"So would I," Kayo said.

"I don't want to hear it again," Lyle said, "especially if it's a ghost."

"Let's watch the rehearsal and listen to all the actors," Rosie said. "If the voice belongs to one of them, we'll know who to stay away from."

"If you don't want to get involved in a mystery," Lyle said, "why search for the voice?"

"The more we know, the safer we are," Kayo said.

Rosie said, "Fact number one: The art museum discovered its Van Gogh painting is a forgery. Fact number two: We found a copy of that same painting hidden where no one would be likely to find it. Fact number three: An unknown voice warned us to stay away from where the painting is."

Lyle nodded.

"We're already involved in a mystery," Rosie said.

Kayo said, "Fact number four: Here we go again."

The girls sat in the auditorium. The voice of the sea captain did not sound like the voice that had warned them to stay away. Neither did the voices of the sailors.

When Lyle danced the hornpipe, Rosie and Kayo applauded. Bone Breath snuggled in Carmen's arms, looking adorable with his pink bow.

In the last scene of Act One all the pirates rushed onstage. Two threatened the ship's captain and his crew with swords as the others searched for the ship's treasure.

Kayo and Rosie leaned forward in their seats, listening carefully to the voices:

"Ahoy, matey. Where's the silver?"

"Run up the Jolly Roger. It's our ship now."

"Your pieces of eight, Captain. Surrender the booty or you'll not live to see the dawn."

The lines were spoken rapidly, one after the next.

"Hand it over, or you'll walk the plank."

At exactly the same moment Kayo and Rosie turned to each other and nodded agreement. From then on, they focused on Chip.

Chapter 9

He sounded the same, Rosie thought. When Chip said, "Hand it over, or you'll walk the plank," his voice was exactly like the voice that had told them to stay away.

Chip had the smallest part in the play. Kayo and Rosie watched and listened, but Chip said nothing else.

As the cast drifted offstage after Act One, Rosie went to claim Bone Breath.

Lyle sat beside Kayo. She whispered, "Chip is the one who told us to stay out. His voice sounds the same."

"Chip couldn't have put the painting there," Lyle said. "This is only his second rehearsal."

Kayo frowned. Had she and Rosie been wrong about the voice?

"Why would Chip care if we go in the storage area?" Lyle said.

"I don't know," Kayo said.

Mrs. Posh stopped Rosie as she led Bone Breath offstage. "Thank you for all the props."

"My dad's making a treasure map," Rosie said.

"Great. Two people found leg-irons. One is a real ball and chain, and one is a fake. The ball on the fake one is hollow; it looks real when it's clamped together, but it isn't heavy." Mrs. Posh smiled. "Two more swords are coming tomorrow," she said, "and Carmen borrowed an old chest from an antiques shop. The only real problem we have now is the skeleton. Norm's sister is a nurse, and she's trying to borrow one from the nursing school."

Impulsively Rosie asked, "Have you known Chip long?"

Mrs. Posh looked surprised. "I just met him yesterday. Why do you ask?"

"I thought I recognized his voice from somewhere else," Rosie said. She considered saying where she thought she had heard the voice, but decided it would be wrong to accuse Chip of anything without proof.

On the way home from rehearsal, Lyle rode in front with his mother. Rosie, Kayo, and Bone Breath rode in back. Partway home, Mrs. Guthrie stopped to buy gas.

Suddenly Lyle said, "Look! That's Charlie!" He pointed at a man who was putting gas into a car at the pump ahead of them.

"Who?" said Rosie.

"Charlie Jennings. The actor who supposedly got called out of town on a family emergency." Lyle opened the door and got out.

Rosie rolled down the window so she and Kayo could hear.

"Hi, Charlie," Lyle said. "We miss you at the theater."

"I hope to be back before opening night," Charlie said.

"I'm sorry about your family emergency."

"Huh?" Charlie said.

"You didn't have to stay out of town very long," Lyle said.

"Oh," Charlie said. "Oh, that. Everything turned out okay." He hung the nozzle back on the pump and replaced the gas cap on his car. "See you later," he said as he walked toward the cashier.

Lyle got back in the car. "He didn't know what I was talking about," Lyle said. "I don't think there was any emergency."

"Why would Mrs. Posh say there was, if it isn't true?" Kayo asked.

"Maybe the painting we found *is* valuable," Rosie said, "and Mrs. Posh and Chip know it.

65

After we found the painting, Mrs. Posh replaced Charlie in the cast temporarily so Chip can be close by until they can do whatever it is they plan to do."

"It would be a lot easier for them to just take the painting somewhere else," Kayo said.

"There must be a reason why it needs to stay at the theater," Lyle said.

"Mrs. Posh said we should move the stack of paintings from behind the curtain to the main part of the storage room," Rosie said. "She wouldn't say that if she was hiding them."

"Maybe Mrs. Posh isn't involved," Lyle said. "Maybe it's Charlie and Chip."

"My head aches from trying to figure this out," Kayo said.

"What do you think we should do now?" Lyle said.

"Nothing," Kayo replied. "We reported the painting we found, we had it checked by experts to be sure it isn't valuable, and we've agreed to stay away from it. Seeing Charlie doesn't change anything."

"For once," said Rosie, "we'll stay out of trouble."

The next morning Rosie, Kayo, and Lyle walked across the school yard together.

"I told my dad about the painting we found," Rosie said.

"What did he say?"

"He said every theater group has a bunch of old paintings."

"Did you tell him about the man who told us to stay away, and about seeing Charlie at the gas station?"

"I started to, but then the phone rang and it was Dad's agent, and I had to get ready for school."

Sammy came across the yard and joined them. "Have you caught the forger yet?" he asked.

Rosie, Kayo, and Lyle stopped walking. They all answered at the same time: "NO!"

"Whoa," said Sammy as he took a step back. Then he scowled at Lyle. "Are *you* in on it with them?" he asked.

"In on what?" Lyle said.

"The club that catches criminals," Sammy said.

"No," Lyle said.

"There isn't any club that catches criminals," Rosie said.

"That's what you always say," said Sammy.

"I told my mom about the contest you won," Kayo said. "She said to tell you not to send them any money."

Sammy scowled.

"Mom said it might be a scam."

"You're just jealous because I won five thousand dollars and you didn't," Sammy said, and he stomped off.

"Wait!" Kayo said.

Sammy turned.

"Mom saw a report on TV about two men who were arrested for mail fraud. They sent letters saying the recipient had won five thousand dollars but needed to send a 'processing fee' of fifteen dollars in order to receive the prize. The men kept all of the 'fees' they got, but never mailed any prize money."

Sammy looked ill. "Did the men live around here?" he asked.

Kayo shook her head. "They were from South Carolina."

"Oh, no," Sammy said. "I've lost three weeks' allowance."

Lyle's dad had a meeting near the theater that night; he offered to drive if the girls didn't mind going early. The theater was locked when they arrived, so they got the hidden key again. They had just let themselves in when they saw Chip parking his car across the street.

"I wonder why Chip is coming so early," Lyle said.

"I don't want to be here alone with him," Kayo said. "I don't trust him."

"The art gallery is still open," Rosie said. "We could go next door and talk to Martha and Helen."

"Chip would see us leave. He might think we came early to snoop behind the curtain," Kayo said.

"Let's sit in the green room until other people come," Lyle said. "Chip doesn't hang out in there with the rest of the cast."

They hurried backstage.

"Maybe Chip came early to get the *Two Cut Sunflowers* painting," Lyle said.

They stopped walking and looked at one another.

"Maybe someone in a forgery ring is meeting him here to pick it up," Rosie said. "Or maybe an unsuspecting person is coming to buy it, thinking it's a real Van Gogh. Maybe it *is* a real Van Gogh, and if we don't stop him, Chip will smuggle it out of the country." Rosie talked faster and faster as she imagined all the possibilities. "Martha and Helen might have been wrong when they said it is not authentic," she said. "Neither of them has good eyesight, and even the experts need to run lab tests."

"We could watch Chip, to see what he does," Kayo said.

"We weren't going to get involved," Lyle said.

"What if it *is* an important painting," Rosie said, "and Chip *is* a crook, and we're the only ones who can stop him?"

"We could hide in the storage room," Lyle said.

"We can crouch down, out of sight," Rosie said, "and if he comes in and takes the painting, we can watch to see what he does with it."

"What if he sees us?" Kayo asked.

"We'll say we were telling ghost stories in the dark," Rosie said.

The children hurried toward the storage room. Bone Breath, sensing their excitement, tugged forward, keeping the leash taut.

"I'm going to shut Bone Breath in the green room," Rosie said. "I'm afraid he'll make noise and give us away."

She opened the green room door and unsnapped Bone Breath's leash. Bone Breath ran straight to the table and began sniffing under it for crumbs. Rosie hung the leash on the doorknob, closed the door, and followed Kayo and Lyle down the hall to the storage room.

They left the door open so they could see if Chip approached. A faint light from the hall spilled through the open doorway, making the props for *Pirate's Plunder* look realistic, and scary. The swords, the leg-irons, the Jolly Roger flag, and the cannon all seemed sinister in the dim light. Rosie shuddered, imagining what it would have been like to be on a ship that was taken over by pirates.

Before they found hiding places, Kayo said, "Look. The skeleton is here."

They approached the skeleton, curious to see it up close. As they looked at it, they heard a slight cough from the hallway. The kids glanced at one another, realizing they should have hidden right away. Now there wasn't time to crouch behind the shelves, away from the door, as they had planned.

The light in the hallway grew brighter.

He was coming. And he was close.

Chapter 10

Lyle ducked behind a rack of costumes.

Rosie and Kayo dropped to their knees beside the cannon. It wasn't a good hiding place, but there was no time to do better.

The light in the doorway grew brighter.

A shadow entered first, long and dark.

Rosie swallowed hard and looked at Kayo.

A man loomed in the doorway, an old-fashioned lantern held high in one hand. A curved sword hung from the man's belt, the sharp steel shining in the lantern light.

The kids stared at the bearded face with a black patch over one eye. Chip.

Rosie knew he was dressed for his part in the play, but that did not lessen her fear. In the play he was a pirate, but what was he in real life?

Why was he here early? What was he looking for? Why had he taken over Charlie's part?

The questions rose into Rosie's mind like bubbles in a soft drink. Why had he ordered them to stay away from behind the curtain? Was the painting they had found merely an old prop? What would Chip do if he found out they had called the police? And what would he do now, if he saw them hiding from him?

Rosie wished someone else were in the theater.

At that moment she was as nervous as if she were really on the deck of an old sailing ship, watching a murderous pirate approach.

Silent and still, they stared at Chip, expecting him to stomp toward them and demand to know why they were hiding in the storage room.

Instead, his glance swept over them, never really looking in their direction. His attention seemed focused on the back of the room, and he didn't look carefully at the front.

He's watching the curtain, Lyle realized. He's checking to see if anyone is back there.

Without turning on the lights, Chip moved quietly toward the back of the room. He stayed on the other side of the metal shelves.

Looking over her shoulder, Kayo could see the back of his head as he parted the green curtain and went behind it. Seconds later he came back out and silently retraced his steps. He stayed

73

close to the far wall and never looked down behind the costumes where the kids were hiding.

When he got back to the open door, Chip continued on out into the hallway, pulling the door
shut behind him, and leaving the three children
in complete darkness.

Rosie and Kayo sagged against each other in
relief. Lyle collapsed on the floor beside them.

"Whew," Lyle said.

"What was he looking for?" Kayo whispered.

"Us," Rosie said. Rosie kept her voice low; Lyle
and Kayo had to lean toward her to hear what she
said. "He's worried that we'll take the painting."

"Why doesn't he take it himself," Kayo said,
"and hide it somewhere else?"

"I think the person who is going to buy the
painting is supposed to meet him at the theater,"
Rosie said, "and with so many people here for
rehearsals, there isn't another good hiding place."

"He could call the buyer," Lyle said, "and ar-
range to meet somewhere else."

"Chip may not know who the buyer is," Kayo
said. "He may be waiting for someone to say a
code word."

"Let's get out of here," Rosie said. "I'll open
the door and make sure he isn't in the hallway.
If I wave, it means he's gone and it's safe to go
to the green room."

"Be careful," Lyle said. "Don't trip on those leg-irons in the dark."

Rosie decided not to take any chances. She crawled toward the door on her hands and knees, feeling carefully the floor in front of her.

Lyle and Kayo stood up, ready to leave when Rosie opened the door and gave the signal.

Rosie was halfway to the door when light suddenly lit up the back of the room. Turning, she saw that the light came from behind the green curtain. Rosie hurried back to Kayo and Lyle.

They stood shoulder to shoulder, hardly daring to breathe, and stared at the light.

It was not a flashlight; it was brighter, and wider.

"I'll bring it out," a voice said. "We keep it hidden, for security reasons."

The kids looked at one another. It was Martha, the art gallery owner.

"Oh, isn't that clever!" cried a woman's voice that the kids did not recognize. "You have a secret door behind that big painting."

So the door does open, Rosie thought. The light is coming from the art gallery. Lyle and Kayo nudged her, and she knew they had realized the same thing.

The light suddenly diminished, as if the door had been pulled partway shut again. The voices grew fainter.

The kids tiptoed closer until they reached the

curtain. By standing right next to it, they could hear what was said in the art gallery.

"It was discovered in an old house that was torn down," Martha said. "Years ago the house was re-modeled and the fireplace wall was covered up. The painting hung over the fireplace, but no one bothered to remove it. They just put up wallboard across the whole thing. When a work crew took down the wall, they found the painting underneath."

"Imagine!" said the unknown voice. "They boarded over a genuine Van Gogh."

"Saints alive!" said Helen.

"It was behind that wall for thirty years," Martha said. "Luckily, the workers brought the painting to us rather than tossing it out with the rest of the wreckage. Of course, we assumed it was only a copy. Still, it was a good copy and we paid them a fair price for it."

Helen continued the story. "When we learned the painting at the Oakwood Art Museum was not original, we had our painting tested by an expert, and that's when we learned that it isn't a copy at all. It's a real Van Gogh."

"I should think you would want to keep it," the woman said.

"We're planning to retire soon," Helen said, "and we need the money. We're willing to take less than its true value because we want it to go to someone who will appreciate it. We went through our customer files and chose you."

"I'm grateful," the woman said. "I never dreamed I would own a painting by Van Gogh."

"Then you'll take it?" Martha asked. "For five hundred thousand dollars?"

Lyle poked Rosie with his elbow.

Kayo's mouth dropped open. She could not imagine anyone having that much money to spend.

"Of course I'll take it. It will use all of my inheritance from my parents, but I'll never have another chance like this."

"It's a good investment," Martha assured her.

"Let me get my checkbook," the woman said.

"I'm afraid we can't take a check, dear," Martha said. "Our accountant insists on cash when the buyer takes the painting."

"What time is it?" the woman asked.

"Six-forty," Helen replied.

"My bank is closed until nine tomorrow morning," the woman said. "I can give you five thousand cash now, to hold the Van Gogh for me, and I'll be back before ten o'clock tomorrow with the balance."

"That will be fine, dear," Martha said.

Rosie, Kayo, and Lyle stayed close to the curtain, hardly able to believe what they were hearing.

The bell over the gallery door jingled, followed by a moment of silence.

Helen said, "I'll be glad to have this deal finished. I've been nervous ever since those kids found our hiding place."

"You worry too much," Martha said. "Those children are so scared of bad vibrations and ghosts they won't come anywhere near this door."

"Next time let's keep the painting in the gallery."

"No," Martha said. "If Prestige Auctions ever accuses you of theft, and the gallery is searched, we don't want them to find any evidence. We're just two little old ladies trying to eke out a living from our love of good art."

"I nearly had a heart attack when those kids walked in and laid the Van Gogh on our counter," Helen said. "What if they hadn't brought it to us? What if they had taken it home? What if they didn't believe that crazy story about a murder?"

Lyle's lips tightened and he clenched his hands into fists. Norm and Dave were right; there was never a murder backstage.

Despicable, thought Rosie, but she didn't get out her vocabulary notebook.

The light grew brighter, and the kids knew the door was fully open again. They heard movement directly behind the curtain.

"We've hidden our paintings here for six years," Martha said, "and nobody ever found one before." She was close now, just on the other side of the curtain.

The children stayed as quiet as the skeleton, waiting for Martha to go back in the gallery and close the door.

"Those kids weren't too bright," Helen said.

We'll see who's bright, Kayo thought. The minute you lock that door, we're going to call the police, and they'll be very interested in what we have to say.

Martha bumped the back of the curtain; dust drifted into the air.

Kayo put her hand over her nose and mouth. She tried not to inhale. Her eyes watered.

Rosie watched her friend, realizing the problem. *Not now*, she thought. *Oh, please, don't sneeze now.*

Kayo's eyes opened wide as she held her breath and pinched her nose with her fingers, but it was no use.

"Ahchoo!"

Even with her hand clamped over her mouth, the sound seemed to blast through the room as if she had sneezed into a microphone.

And then, to make it even worse, Kayo sneezed again.

Chapter 11

The green curtain billowed out, pushed from the other side.

Rosie, Kayo, and Lyle backed away from it, watching the place where the two sides met.

Martha burst through the opening, without her walker. She stood straight, her shoulders back.

"You!" she said, glaring at the children.

For an instant nobody moved. The moment seemed frozen in time, as if someone had hit the Pause button on a videotape.

"You heard us, didn't you?" she demanded.

No one answered.

Helen rushed into the storage room.

"They were back here, listening," Martha said. "They know everything."

As she spoke she strode past the astonished

children, turned on the light, and looked quickly around the storage room.

Rosie, Kayo, and Lyle gawked at her, realizing that Martha was perfectly able to walk alone. And Helen was not a sweet, kindly art lover, but a coldhearted crook.

Rosie's breath came fast. Maybe we can talk our way out of this, she thought. We have to make them believe we didn't hear.

"We just got here," Rosie said. "We're helping with props."

"We were looking at the skeleton," Lyle said. He pointed to it. "We didn't hear you talking; we didn't even know you were back there."

"Are you helping with props, too?" Kayo asked, trying to sound curious. "Is that why you're here?"

Helen looked uncertain, but Martha's eyes were cold.

"We can use the help," Kayo said.

"We still need another sword," Lyle said.

Martha shook her head as she listened. "Save your breath," she said as she reached for the zipper on her hip purse.

As soon as Rosie saw Martha's hand on the zipper, she said, "We have to go now. The rehearsal starts in a few minutes."

She bolted toward the door, with Kayo and Lyle beside her.

"Help!" Kayo yelled. She wondered if anyone besides Chip had arrived yet. Even if they had, she wasn't sure they would hear her. If people were chatting in the green room or out in the auditorium seats, they probably would not hear her with the storage room door shut. If Chip heard her call, would he come to help? Or would he help Martha and Helen?

"Stop right there," Martha said. She took a small handgun from her purse and pointed it at the kids. "You aren't going anywhere." Her voice sounded sinister, the way the pirates sounded in the play when they threatened to kill the sea captain.

Kayo looked at the gun; she didn't yell anymore.

"Come this way," Martha said.

Kayo, Lyle, and Rosie walked slowly toward her.

Martha's eyes darted around the room. "Helen," she said. "See if you can lift that ball and chain. We need to be sure these kids don't get away."

Helen walked to the real ball and chain and tried to pick it up. "It's too heavy," she said. She pulled on the chain, trying to drag the ball across the floor, but she couldn't move it.

"You help her," Martha said, nodding at Lyle.

"Right," Lyle said, but instead of going to the ball and chain that Helen was trying to lift, he went to the fake one. He grasped the chain and then, pretending to struggle with all his might, he pulled the ball across the floor.

Rosie thought, No wonder he got a part in the play. He's a terrific actor.

"Take it behind the curtain," Martha instructed. "Put it in the gallery. Helen, hold the curtain aside so I can make sure he comes right back."

Helen pulled the curtain back.

Kayo sneezed again.

The door behind the curtain was wide open; Rosie and Kayo could see straight into the art gallery.

Lyle dragged the fake ball and chain into the gallery.

As soon as it was past the door, Martha said, "Now come back and get the other one."

Lyle straightened up and pretended to wipe his brow. He glanced at the gallery door, trying to see if he could dash out of Martha's line of sight and get away.

"Don't try to run for it," Martha said, "unless you want your friends to be hurt."

Lyle returned to the storage room and tried to pull the real ball and chain across the floor. It didn't move.

"I'm all worn out from the first one," Lyle said. "I can't pull this one, too."

83

"Help him," Martha said to Helen.

Helen grasped the chain next to Lyle's hand and tugged. Together they were able to drag the real ball and chain across the floor.

When Helen and Lyle reached the opening in the curtain, Martha spoke to Kayo and Rosie. "Follow them," she said.

Helen and Lyle pulled the ball and chain behind the curtain, through the open door, and into the art gallery.

Rosie and Kayo followed, with Martha and the gun right behind them.

As soon as they were all in the gallery, Helen locked the door that opened to the street. She set a CLOSED sign in the window and turned off all the gallery lights except a small lamp on the desk behind the counter.

Martha pulled the door to the theater shut and locked it. Helen pushed the large painting back in place, covering the door.

A faint light from the street lamp outside shone in through the window. Kayo saw Mrs. Posh walk past the gallery toward the theater. Mrs. Posh did not look in the window, and Kayo did not dare call out. Not with the gun still in Martha's hand.

"Those balls and chains weigh a ton," Helen said as she rubbed the small of her back.

"Good," Martha said. "We have to be sure

these kids don't talk to anyone until after we get the money."

Helen put one hand on her head and removed all of her white hair.

The kids stared at her. She wasn't an elderly woman at all; she was a young woman in a white wig.

"This thing always makes my head itch," Helen said as she scratched her scalp.

"You girls stand here," Martha said, "next to the leg-irons."

Kayo and Rosie did as she directed.

"Put the leg-irons on them," Martha said.

Helen knelt on the floor and clamped the thick iron collar of the real ball and chain around Rosie's ankle. A heavy chain connected the collar to the iron ball. Rosie tried to lift her foot; she could not.

Lyle pretended he thought Martha was talking to him. He quickly knelt beside Kayo and clamped the fake ball and chain on Kayo's ankle.

Way to go, Lyle, Kayo thought. She knew she would easily be able to move with the hollow ball clamped to her leg.

"Get the padlock from the safe," Martha said, "and lock the two chains together."

"They can't walk anywhere now," Helen said. "And all our records are in the safe."

"If these kids get loose," Martha said, "there will be a dozen cops at our door."

"Birdie will see the kids when she brings the money tomorrow morning."

"No, she won't."

Helen frowned but didn't argue. She walked to a large safe in the far corner of the room and dialed some numbers on a heavy padlock. When the padlock sprang open, she removed it from the safe and carried it to the girls. She stuck the open end of the padlock through a link in Rosie's chain and then reached for Kayo's chain.

The three children watched, knowing that if Helen picked up the chain that hung from Kayo's ankle, she would find out how light it was. She would know Lyle had tricked her.

But instead of picking the chain up, Helen stuck the padlock through one link, and pushed on the two ends of the padlock.

Click. The padlock snapped closed.

Rosie and Kayo looked down. Kayo tried to lift her foot, but it was now weighted down by the real ball and chain, just as Rosie's foot was. There was no way she would be able to walk now. Lyle's quick thinking and smart acting were wasted.

"What about him?" Helen said, nodding toward Lyle.

"We'll use rope for him," Martha said.

Backstage Fright

Rosie glanced at her watch. People are arriving for rehearsal, she thought. They will find Bone Breath in the green room and wonder why he is there alone. They'll look for us.

Hope fought with despair in Rosie's mind as she realized, *They'll look for us, but they won't look here.*

Chapter

12

ℒie down," Helen said to Lyle, "on your stomach."

When Lyle was on the floor, Helen tied his hands behind his back with rope. Then she tied his feet together and wound the end of the rope around a leg of the safe before she knotted it.

Lyle clenched his teeth, forcing himself to lie still. He wanted to shove the rope out of her hands and run away, but he knew it would be foolish not to do exactly what she said. As long as Martha held the gun, he had to obey the women.

While Helen tied Lyle to the safe, Martha made a phone call. She laid the receiver on the counter and pushed the numbers. With her other hand, she kept the gun aimed at Rosie and Kayo. "Stay quiet," she warned as she put the receiver to her ear.

"Hello, Mrs. Bird?" Martha said. "This is Martha from the gallery. We've decided to bring the Van Gogh to your bank tomorrow morning and make our transaction there. Yes, dear. We don't like the idea of you driving alone with so much cash. This will be safer for you." There was a slight pause. "Oh, you're welcome, dear. Just tell me which bank and we'll wait for you in the parking lot. We'll have the painting in our car."

Martha wrote something on the notepad that was next to the telephone. "Oh, by the way," she said, "I advise you not to mention your purchase to anyone. Some art collectors would do most anything to own the painting you are buying. For your own security, you should keep quiet about it. I'd feel terrible if your home got robbed."

After Martha hung up she tore the top paper from the notepad and put it in her hip purse.

Rosie expected Helen to tie her hands and Kayo's hands, after Helen finished tying Lyle. Instead, Helen laid the remaining rope on the floor.

"I'm hungry," Helen said. "I'm going to go get sandwiches and bring them back here."

"We can stop on the way home," Martha said.

"We can't go home," Helen said. "What about these kids? We can't leave them here."

"We're going to leave everything here," Martha said, "and start over in a new city."

Helen groaned. "Not again. I hate moving."

"There isn't much choice this time, is there? As soon as these kids are found, they'll spill the whole story."

"We could do away with them."

A shiver slid down the back of Rosie's neck. She reached for Kayo's hand.

Martha did not answer immediately. Finally she said, "How?"

"You're holding a gun," Helen said.

Kayo took off her Seattle Mariners cap, smoothed her hair back, and replaced the cap.

"No," Martha said. "It doesn't bother me to take money from fools like Birdie who believe anything we tell them. But it would bother me to use the gun." Martha looked at Rosie and Kayo. "Don't get me wrong," she said. "I'll use it if I have to."

Kayo blinked the tears out of her eyes.

"Where do you plan to go this time?" Helen asked.

"How does Florida sound?"

"Terrible."

"There are lots of wealthy old folks in Florida," Martha said. "Some of them will be art collectors."

Helen opened the safe and removed several file folders.

"You won't get away," Rosie said. "We already called the police and told them about the painting we found."

"You're lying," Martha said. "If you had called the cops, they would be here by now."

"We called them two days ago," Lyle said. As soon as he said *two days ago*, he knew it was a mistake. "They've been watching this place ever since," he added.

"If the cops were called two days ago and they have not made a move yet," Helen said, "you can bet they don't plan to do anything. They probably thought it was a prank call."

"We need gags," Martha said, "so they can't yell for help after we leave."

Helen unpinned her brooch and removed the shawl that was draped around her shoulders. She opened a drawer, found a large pair of scissors, and cut the shawl into three triangular pieces. She tied one piece tightly around Lyle's mouth. Then she tied one around Kayo's mouth and one around Rosie's.

While the gags were being put on, Kayo and Rosie kept their arms tight against their sides, hoping the women would not think about tying their hands.

If our hands are free, Kayo thought, we'll be

able to remove the gags and call for help as soon as Martha and Helen leave.

When the three kids were gagged, Helen moved the huge painting that hid the door to the theater. She unlocked the door.

"I hate leaving *Stop Light* behind," Helen said. "That's my favorite painting."

Rosie looked at the splotches of red, yellow, and green paint on the huge canvas. She wondered how that could possibly be anyone's favorite painting. It looked to her like something a three-year-old would do.

"You never did have any taste in art," Martha said.

Helen opened the door, stepped through, and returned with *Two Cut Sunflowers* under her arm. She locked the door, pushed *Stop Light* back into place, and slipped the Van Gogh painting into a large plastic bag.

Helen turned off the desk lamp. "Let's go," she said.

Martha put the gun in her hip purse.

Both women looked cautiously out the window before they opened the front door.

"Wait," Martha said. "Someone's coming."

They stood together behind the door, peering out the front window where several paintings were displayed.

From where Rosie and Kayo stood at the back

of the gallery, they could also see out the window. They watched Norm, Dean, and Dave walk along the sidewalk toward the theater. The men were only a few yards away.

Since Martha and Helen had their backs to the girls, Rosie and Kayo waved their arms over their heads, trying to attract the men's attention.

The actors talked and laughed as they walked along; they didn't glance toward the dark gallery. After a few seconds the street outside was empty again. Kayo and Rosie dropped their hands to their sides.

Martha punched some numbers into what was apparently a burglar alarm system. She looked carefully around the gallery, the way Rosie's parents always examined a hotel room before they checked out, to be sure they weren't leaving something behind. Martha's eyes stopped on the piece of rope. "Did you tie the girls?" she asked.

"They don't need to be tied," Helen said. "They have chains on their legs."

"We still have to tie their hands," Martha said. "Otherwise, they'll have those gags off before we're a block away."

"Oh," said Helen. She picked up the rope and quickly wrapped it around Rosie, tying her hands to her sides. She did the same with Kayo.

"I really don't want to move to Florida, or anywhere else," Helen said as she opened the door.

"Neither do I," Martha said, "but . . ."

"It wouldn't bother *me* to use the gun," Helen said. "I'll take you home and come back by myself."

The children did not hear Martha's reply. She pulled the door closed, and the two women walked away.

Chapter
13

Where's my itty-bitty sweetums doggie-pie?"
Carmen said as she entered the green room.

Bone Breath ran to her, wagging his tail.

"There's my sweet baby," Carmen said. She
looked around the room. "Where is your person?"
she asked the dog.

Bone Breath licked Carmen's shoe.

"The dog was in here alone when I arrived,"
Norm said. "The girls probably went to comb
their hair."

"Did those naughty girls leave the baby doggie
here all by her lonesome?" Carmen cried. She
picked Bone Breath up. "Oh, you poor little darling. You just come here and let Carmen comfort
you." Carmen kissed Bone Breath's head, over
and over.

Norm held out his arms. "I'm here all alone," he said. "Don't you want to comfort me?"

"You aren't cute and fuzzy," Carmen said as she carried Bone Breath out of the green room and prepared to make her entrance onstage.

When Bone Breath's scene was finished, Carmen took him back to the green room. It was empty. Frowning, she walked through the backstage area, looking for Rosie and Kayo. When there was a break between scenes, Carmen asked Mrs. Posh if she knew where the girls were.

"I haven't seen them," Mrs. Posh replied. "Lyle isn't here, either. He missed his part at the end of Scene One."

"You know how kids are," Dean said. "They probably went out for a pizza and forgot the time."

"They've always been reliable before," Mrs. Posh said. "Did you look in the storage room? Maybe they're working on that mermaid."

"I looked there," Carmen said. "The light was on, but the room was empty."

"They'll show up," Norm said. "They have to come back to get their dog."

Carmen put Bone Breath in the green room. When she turned to leave, Bone Breath scampered past her into the hallway.

"Daisy!" Carmen said. "Get back here."

Bone Breath, his nose to the floor, headed down the hall toward the storage room.

Carmen hurried after him. "Now, sweetums," Carmen said. "You have to wait in the green room. You can't be running loose in the theater."

Bone Breath went straight to the storage room door. He sniffed the bottom of the door and whined. He pawed at the door.

"You silly dog," Carmen said. "What's wrong with you? Why do you want to go in there?"

Bone Breath whined and pawed some more.

Carmen opened the door and Bone Breath dashed in. He sniffed the floor, walking back and forth. He stopped and sniffed the toes of the skeleton. Then he headed for the back of the room and ducked underneath the green curtain.

"No, no," Carmen said as she hurried after him. "Come back here."

Bone Breath kept his nose to the floor. He stood next to the locked door to the gallery and pawed at it, the same way he had pawed at the storage room door.

Carmen pushed through the opening in the curtain. "There is nothing back here," she scolded. She picked Bone Breath up. He twisted, trying to jump down, but she held on firmly and marched out of the storage room.

"Naughty, naughty," she said. "You mustn't run away from Carmen again."

97

As she left the storage room, Chip walked down the hall toward her. "Hi, Carmen," he said. "What are you doing back here?"

"This silly dog ran away from me," Carmen said. "She was pawing the wall at the back of the storage room."

"Where?" Chip asked.

"She ran under that old curtain that hangs on the back wall," Carmen said. "I had to go back there after her. Those girls know better than to leave their dog here alone."

"Where are the girls?" Chip asked.

"We don't know, and it makes me very cross. I have a costume change to make; I can't take care of their dog for them between scenes."

"I'll watch the dog for you," Chip said.

Carmen handed Bone Breath to Chip. "See that you have her in the green room before the start of Act Two," she said.

Chip didn't answer. He carried Bone Breath into the storage room, put him down, and closed the door.

Bone Breath raced to the back of the room and went under the green curtain.

Rosie and Kayo watched Helen and Martha through the window until they were out of sight.

"Ummm," said Rosie. It was so frustrating not to be able to talk.

Lyle tried to roll out from behind the counter so he could see the girls, but the safe was an anchor.

Rosie tried to slide her chained foot forward, hoping Kayo would do the same. If we work together, she thought, maybe we'll be strong enough to pull the heavy ball across the floor. If we can get close to the window, someone might look in and notice us.

Kayo realized Rosie was trying to slide her foot forward, so she tried to slide her foot, too, but the ball was too heavy. All the girls succeeded in doing was rubbing their skin raw where the iron clasps surrounded their ankles.

Discouraged, Rosie and Kayo stopped struggling and tried to think what else they could do. Rosie wondered how much time they had before Helen returned. An hour? Less? Oakwood was not a big city; you could drive from one side to the other in less than thirty minutes.

"Yip!"

The sound was muffled by the closed door, but the kids recognized Bone Breath's bark.

"Ummm," Rosie said again.

Kayo and Lyle made groaning sounds, too, hoping Bone Breath would hear them. If the dog kept barking at the locked door, perhaps someone would leave the theater and come to the art gallery, to see what was on the other side of the door.

The bark was barely out of Bone Breath's mouth when Chip reached the locked door. Chip looked at the framed pictures that still leaned against the wall. He took a cellular phone from his back pocket and made a call.

As he talked, he ran out of the storage room, closing the door behind him so Bone Breath couldn't get out.

Chip dashed past the set construction and the green room, and cut across the far side of the stage. He waved at Mrs. Posh, who nodded, and then he ran up the aisle and out the door of the theater.

He went straight to his car.

From inside the gallery, Rosie and Kayo saw Chip run to his car, still wearing the pirate costume.

Rosie wondered if Helen had called him and told him her intention. Maybe she doesn't want to use the gun in the gallery, Rosie thought. Maybe Chip is going to help her take us someplace else, where gunshots won't be heard.

From where Lyle lay on the floor, he could not see out the window. But he could see the scissors that Helen had used to make the gags. She had left them on the seat of the desk chair.

Lyle twisted around until his head was under the chair. He had to stretch forward; the rope between his feet and the safe was pulled taut.

He slid his legs sideways and rolled onto his back. Then he sat up, butting the top of his head against the bottom of the chair. The chair tilted. The scissors slid forward and dropped onto the floor beside Lyle's chest.

Lyle lowered his head, easing the chair legs back down. He rolled onto his side, so his hands were next to the scissors. Helen had tied his wrists together, but his fingers could still move.

Lyle lay awkwardly on his side as his fingers felt the floor behind him, searching for the scissors. All those stretching exercises for dance class are paying off, Lyle thought. I'm bending in ways that most people would not be able to bend.

At last one hand touched metal. Lyle pushed the blades of the scissors open. Holding tight to the place where the blades joined, he sawed one blade across the rope that tied his wrists. Back and forth, back and forth. The rope was thick, the scissors were not very sharp, and he could only move the blade two inches. Back and forth, back and forth; Lyle continued to saw.

His hand soon ached, from holding the scissors at such an odd angle, and he knew if the scissors slipped off the rope, he would cut himself.

Rosie tried to figure out a way to move. The

ball was too heavy to pull with one leg. But maybe, she thought, if we sit down, we can push the ball across the floor.

Rosie sat on the floor. Kayo looked at her with questioning eyes. Rosie nodded her head, yes, and Kayo sat beside her.

Rosie scooted on her bottom, positioning herself so the ball was in front of her foot. Then she slid forward, bending her knees.

Kayo followed Rosie's lead. When their knees were nearly to their chins, Rosie positioned her feet on the heavy ball.

Now Kayo understood Rosie's idea, and she put her right foot on the ball, too. The edge of her shoe covered the edge of Rosie's left shoe. There wasn't room on the ball for Kayo's other foot, so she put it against the thick chain. Pushing the chain forward would help move the ball.

"Uh," said Rosie.

Both girls shoved as hard as they could. The ball slid a few inches. The girls scooted forward and shoved again. By leaning backward, they could brace their hands on the floor and push harder.

"Yip! Yip, yip, yip!" Bone Breath continued to bark on the other side of the door. Lyle wondered why no one looked to see what he was barking at.

The girls pushed again. And again. Each time the ball moved an inch or two.

Rosie's legs soon ached. Kayo was stronger because she exercised daily with ankle weights as part of her training to be a professional baseball player. Both girls kept pushing until they had moved the ball close to the front door of the gallery.

At that point Kayo started to slide sideways, to aim toward the window. She thought they were trying to get close to the window, so that someone might look in and see them.

But Rosie said, "Ummm," and shook her head. Instead of going toward the window, Rosie nodded her head toward the door, indicating that they should shove the iron ball against it.

Kayo frowned. She didn't think there was any chance that she and Rosie could break the door down by pushing the ball against it with their feet. But she had learned long ago that Rosie often had good ideas, and she decided to do what Rosie wanted.

When the ball was against the door, Rosie said, "Umm." Both girls shoved as hard as they could. The heavy ball clunked against the door. Rosie and Kayo shoved again. *Clunk!*

Clunk. Clunk. Clunk.

The girls got into a rhythm, bending their knees and then pushing on the ball. Each time the ball hit the door, the door jiggled a little.

Each time Rosie hoped the burglar alarm would go off.

After two straight minutes of pushing as hard and fast as they could, Rosie had to rest. She sat back, straightened her legs, and looked up through the gallery window.

Helen was back.

Chapter

14

*F*ear sent new strength into Rosie's legs. She and Kayo pushed the ball again, harder than ever. *Clunk! Clunk!* The wood splintered, the door shook, and the burglar alarm went off.

Whooo, whooo, whooo. The loud siren screeched through the night.

Startled by the sudden noise, Lyle dropped the scissors.

Rosie and Kayo watched the doorknob turn. The iron ball prevented the door from opening more than a few inches, but that was far enough for Helen to stick her hand in and push the button that turned off the burglar alarm. The siren stopped.

"Is anyone coming?" Helen said. "Did they hear the alarm?"

The girls wondered who was with her. They had thought Helen would return alone.

"No. It wasn't on long enough." The voice was Martha's. "Anyone who heard it probably thinks it was a fire truck going past."

"Help me open the door," Helen said. "They've managed to push something heavy up against it."

The iron ball slid toward Rosie as the door slowly opened. Martha and Helen slipped inside and closed the door behind them. Martha looked down at Rosie and Kayo. Helen hurried behind the counter to check on Lyle.

"You're smarter than I gave you credit for," Martha said.

"This one got hold of the scissors," Helen said. "He's cut nearly all the way through the rope on his wrists. Another five minutes and he would have had his hands free."

"Another five minutes," Martha said, "and the cops would have come to see why the burglar alarm was on."

"It's a good thing we came back," Helen said.

"I had thought it would bother me to get rid of these kids," Martha said. "But it won't. Not now."

Carmen went into the green room to get Bone Breath for their second scene together. The girls were not there, and neither was the dog. Chip wasn't there, either.

Feeling irritated at all of them, Carmen walked to the storage room. The minute she opened the door, she heard the barking. She hurried to the back of the room and went behind the curtain. "Stop that!" she said. "No, no."

Bone Breath's tail drooped down and he hung his head.

Carmen picked him up. "What is the matter with you?" she scolded. "You've been such a good doggie until now."

She carried Bone Breath out of the storage room, wondering why the little dog was suddenly misbehaving. For that matter, she thought, why are those girls suddenly misbehaving? They've been so dependable; it really wasn't like them to go off and leave the dog unattended. It wasn't like Lyle to miss his hornpipe dance, either.

Carmen stopped walking. Maybe, she thought, something has happened to them.

She listened to the voices coming from on-stage. She didn't want to disrupt the rehearsal, but she felt very uneasy.

She went into the green room, where the cast list was posted. It had the names, addresses, and telephone numbers of everyone who was helping with *Pirate's Plunder.* Carmen ran her finger down the list until she found the props crew.

Then she picked up the telephone and dialed Kayo's number.

The line was busy.

Carmen dialed Rosie's number. Mrs. Saunders answered. Carmen explained who she was and said the girls were not at rehearsal. "The little dog is here," Carmen said, "but we have not seen the girls or Lyle all evening."

"Something is wrong," Mrs. Saunders said. "Rosie would never leave the theater without permission. Please watch Bone Breath until we can get there."

Carmen hung up the phone and patted Bone Breath. "This doesn't sound good, little sweetums," she said. "This doesn't sound good at all."

Bone Breath leaned against Carmen and whined.

Mrs. Saunders immediately dialed the police. When Mr. Saunders heard what his wife was telling the police, he dropped the book he had been reading and grabbed his car keys. As soon as she hung up, they raced out the door and headed toward the theater. As Mrs. Saunders drove, Mr. Saunders called Kayo's mother on the car phone. He asked her to call Lyle's parents.

Helen untied Lyle's feet and used the rope to retie his hands. She instructed him to stand beside Rosie and Kayo. Meanwhile, Martha opened the padlock and removed it.

With the padlock gone, Kayo knew she would be able to run, if she got the chance. But with her hands still tied, she had no way to open the door.

"Maybe we should do it right here and now," Helen said, "instead of driving them out into the country."

"Someone might hear the shots."

"Someone might see them get into the car, too."

"On this street?" Martha said. "There's nobody here at night except the theater group, and their rehearsals never end before ten."

Helen unlocked the heavy ball and chain that was attached to Rosie's ankle. She started to unlock the chain on Kayo's ankle and then bent and examined it closely. She picked up the fake ball and held it in one hand.

"They tricked us," she said. "This ball is light as a sponge. If we had not used the padlock, she could easily have walked away."

Martha glared at the children.

They shrank back from the anger in her eyes.

Rosie listened for Bone Breath, but she no longer heard any barking.

Martha took the gun from her purse again. "We're going to walk quietly out the door," she said. "My car is parked directly in front of the gallery. Get in the backseat and don't do anything to make noise." She moved close to the children, until she stood directly behind them.

Rosie, Kayo, and Lyle looked at one another. Rosie's eyes flashed angrily. She knew it was risky to try to jump Martha and knock the gun away, but if they didn't do something, their lives were going to end soon. It's better, she thought, to try to escape than to get herded into the car like a bunch of sheep.

Seeing the look on Rosie's face, Kayo's heart began to race. Rosie's going to try to get away, Kayo thought. She narrowed her eyes and stared at Lyle, hoping he would catch on. *Be ready*, she wanted to tell him. *If we think fast and move together, we might make it.*

Lyle saw the way Kayo looked at him and knew she was trying to send him a message. He had no clue what the message was, but he had already decided that as soon as they got outside, he would fling himself at Martha and try to knock the gun out of her hand. If he succeeded, Rosie and Kayo might be able to run into the theater before Martha or Helen could pick the gun up.

If I miss, Lyle thought, Martha might shoot right there on the sidewalk. If she does, she'll get caught for sure. Of course, he realized miserably, we'll be just as dead, whether she's caught or not.

Backstage Fright

Helen opened the door.

Chip stood on the other side, a gun in his hand.

Rosie, Kayo, and Lyle felt as if they'd just been kicked in the stomach. All three had been geared up to try to make a break, and now they knew they couldn't do it. Not with two guns aimed at them.

Chapter 15

Oakwood Police," Chip said. "Throw the gun down and put your hands in the air."

"Oh, you actors," Martha said. "Always playing a role."

Chip kept the gun aimed at Martha. With his other hand he removed identification from his pocket and held it toward Helen.

"Saints alive!" Helen said. "It's a cop in a pirate costume."

"Toss the gun down," Chip said. "Now."

Martha dropped the gun on the ground at Chip's feet. "We caught these children in the art gallery," she said. "We think they broke in and stole a valuable painting."

Two police cars pulled up to the curb. Officer Ken Bremner got out of one. He looked at

Rosie, Kayo, and Lyle. "I might have known," he said.

Two female officers got out of the other patrol car. They quickly untied the three gags.

As soon as Rosie's gag was removed, she said, "These women have a Vincent Van Gogh painting in their car. We don't know if it's genuine or a forgery, but a Mrs. Bird is going to give them five hundred thousand dollars cash for it tomorrow morning."

Chip began to read Martha and Helen their rights.

Officer Bremner looked in the car and saw the painting of *Two Cut Sunflowers*. "I thought you weren't trying to catch the forger," he said.

"We didn't do it on purpose," Kayo said.

"I'm sure you didn't."

Rosie, Kayo, and Lyle grinned at him.

All the parents arrived. While two officers drove Martha and Helen to the police station to get booked, everyone else went into the theater to hear what had happened.

"I'm an undercover agent," Chip explained. "When you called to say you'd found the painting, I was sent to check into it. I showed it to the director of the Oakwood Art Museum, and she said it was either the original Van Gogh or an excellent copy. We assumed someone from the theater had hidden the painting in the storage

113

room, but we didn't know who or why. I arranged with Mrs. Posh to give me a small part, so there was a reason for me to hang around backstage whenever the theater was occupied."

"Are you the one who warned us to stay away?" Lyle asked.

"Yes. I knew the real culprit would not make a move if you kids were there. I couldn't let you know my identity; I needed to keep the whole plan secret or it would not work."

"What tipped you off that we were in the art gallery now?" Rosie asked.

"The burglar alarm," Officer Bremner said. "First Chip reported that the painting was gone and that three children in the cast had left the theater."

"I thought you kids took it," Chip said. "I was on my way to talk to your parents."

"Before he got there," Officer Bremner said, "Mrs. Saunders called to say you were missing. I told Chip to go back and cruise the area around the theater and look for you. Then the burglar alarm went off. Even though the alarm didn't run long, the gallery is next door to the theater. It seemed an odd coincidence so I called Chip again and asked him to check it out."

"As I approached the gallery," Chip said, "I heard voices inside. I thought I was going to interrupt a burglary in progress, so I drew my gun."

"We thought you hid the painting," Rosie said.
"Or maybe you and Charlie together," Lyle
said.

Chip shook his head. "Charlie cooperated fully
with the police by letting me play his role. That's
his only involvement."

"Daisy barked and barked at that door," Carmen said. "She tried to tell us where the children
were and we didn't pay any attention, did we,
little sweetums?" She leaned down and made
kissing sounds in front of Bone Breath's face.
"Darling Daisy is a hero."

"That's true," Chip said. "The dog led me to
where the painting had been stored, and that's
how I discovered it was gone. I checked when I
got to the theater tonight, and it was there then."

"You really should have told an adult about
that painting," Mrs. Benton said to Kayo.

"We did," Kayo said. "We told the police. And
we told Mrs. Posh. We told Martha and Helen,
too. They all said the painting was only an old
prop."

"I'm sorry about that," Mrs. Posh said. "I never
dreamed it would be anything else until Chip
contacted me."

"We didn't know Martha and Helen were
lying," Lyle said.

"Rosie started to tell me," Mr. Saunders said,
"but we got interrupted."

"We really meant to stay out of this," Rosie said. "But when we thought an innocent person was going to be bilked out of a lot of money, we eavesdropped despite our good intentions. I guess we got carried away."

"I can't imagine that," Mr. Saunders said.

Officer Bremner asked Rosie, Kayo, Lyle, and their parents to meet him in his office at five-thirty the next day. Chip was there, too.

When everyone had arrived, Officer Bremner said, "I wanted you to hear the end of the story before we release it to the press. The painting you found is the original Van Gogh."

The parents gasped.

Rosie's mouth dropped open. She and Kayo stared at each other.

"No wonder I liked it," Lyle said.

"After examining the files that were in Martha and Helen Antwerp's car, we flew the painting to Dr. Claude Montfort, an art historian in Paris. He confirmed that it was the same painting he tested two years ago for Prestige Auctions."

"I don't understand," Kayo said.

"Helen works part-time for Prestige Auctions, using a different name. In the last six years Prestige had eleven valuable paintings verified by experts. In each case Helen switched those paintings for forgeries done by Martha. The forgeries were then sold at auction as originals, complete with certificates of authenticity, while the real originals were sold by the Antwerp sisters to private collectors."

"How despicable," said Rosie as she opened her notebook.

"Martha pleaded innocent to all charges," Officer Bremner said, "but Helen gave a full confession. She stated that her sister copies the famous paintings, covers them with dirty varnish to make them look old, and creates crackling by alternately baking and freezing them."

"If she can paint well enough to fool the art museum into thinking her painting was done by Van Gogh," Lyle said, "I should think she would want to do her own work and sign her name to it."

"Her own name wouldn't bring five hundred thousand dollars," said Chip.

"What a waste of talent," Mrs. Saunders said.

"You held an original Van Gogh painting in your hands," Mr. Saunders said. "Not many people ever do that."

"I not only held it," Rosie said, "I sat on it."

"We are lucky Chip was close by last night," Officer Bremner said. "A lot of money was involved. On the way to the jail Martha said she should have shot you, instead of tying you up."

Mrs. Saunders reached for Rosie's hand and held it.

"I thought getting sued for breaking into that man's car was the worst thing that could happen to us," Mrs. Benton said, "but I was wrong. This could have been much worse. We could have lost you."

"I'm sorry, Mom," Kayo said. "I don't mean to be so much trouble to you."

"The lawsuit about the broken window has been dropped," Mrs. Saunders said. "I spoke with the attorney for the dog's owner just before I left work to come here. After volunteers from People for the Ethical Treatment of Animals threatened to picket his office, he decided it would be in his best interest not to sue anybody."

"There's one part I still don't understand," Lyle said to Officer Bremner. "When you arrived last night, you said, 'I might have known,' as if you weren't surprised to see us."

"I meant the girls."

Lyle looked at Rosie and Kayo. "Sammy said you had a club that helps the police, but I thought he was making it up."

"He was," Kayo said. "We have a club that helps animals."

Officer Bremner chuckled. "And that's why you were in the art gallery with a forger and a thief," he said.

"Setting off the burglar alarm," added Chip.

"We'll explain about Care Club later," Rosie told Lyle.

"One good thing has come of all this," Kayo said. "We have plenty of information about art forgery for our school reports."

Rosie rubbed her sore ankle, where the collar from the ball and chain had scraped it raw. "There must be an easier way to do research," she said.

"There must be an easier way to raise children," Mrs. Saunders said, and the other parents agreed.

About the Author

Peg Kehret's popular novels for young people are regularly nominated for state awards. She has received the Young Hoosier Award, the Golden Sower Award, the Iowa Children's Choice Award, the Sequoyah Award, the Celebrate Literacy Award, the Pacific Northwest Young Reader's Choice Award, the Maud Hart Lovelace Award, and the New Mexico Land of Enchantment Award. She lives with her husband, Carl, and their animal friends in Washington State, where she is a volunteer at The Humane Society and SPCA. Her two grown children and four grandchildren live in Washington, too.

Peg's Minstrel titles include *Nightmare Mountain; Sisters, Long Ago; Cages; Terror at the Zoo; Horror at the Haunted House;* and the *Frightmares*™ series.